The Earth's Project

Starship—Cosmic Mall

The Earth's Project

D. A. Tuskey

Alpharetta, GA

This is a work of fiction. Names, characters, businesses, places, and events are either the products of the author's imagination or are used in a fictitious manner. Any resemblance to actual persons, living or dead, or actual events is purely coincidental.

ISBN: 978-1-6653-0093-3 - Paperback
eISBN: 978-1-6653-0094-0 - ePub

Printed in the United States of America 1 1 0 5 2 1

∞This paper meets the requirements of ANSI/NISO Z39.48-1992 (Permanence of Paper)

Author photo by Sarah Tuskey

Original drawing of the Starship *Cosmic Mall* by Jonathan Carpenter

I couldn't imagine dedicating this book to anyone but my wonderful wife,
Sarah.
She saw the story in my overnight dream even before I did.
She encouraged me to continue when I was ready to quit.
And of all the "out of this world" ideas, the A deck was her inspiration.

Thank you, My Love

Chapter 1

Mac

Mac awoke just before dawn on what would prove to be a crisp but clear early spring day in the year 2217. Although she thoroughly enjoyed all of the new science she was learning at the Galactic School of Science and Technology, her previous night's sleep had not been sound.

The school was set in a small cove of a Catskill Mountain valley in upstate New York. Consisting of several red brick buildings that were about 150 years old, the campus's two largest buildings housed classrooms and laboratories, while four smaller ones served as administrative offices, offices for tenured professors, and private labs. Several other moderately sized buildings of concrete, glass, and a more recent building material known as monolight—one-third the weight but twice the strength of conventional cement—served as dormitories.

For all four years of her schooling, she had shared her dorm room with a midwestern girl from Indiana named Stella Steel, who was some years older than Mac. Stella was there to study botany and alien horticulture.

Mac was rubbing the sleep out of her eyes when she heard Stella say from under the covers of her bed, "I told you that extra piece of Gullroodian pizza would give you nightmares. How many times have I said that earthlings can't have more than two pieces of that stuff when it's been peppered with Colodin spice berries?"

"I didn't have any nightmares, and I only ate one slice of pizza," said Mac. "And besides, as I recall, it was *you* who ate not only a third but also a fourth slice of that alien excuse for an Italian masterpiece. So, I'm guessing you had the nightmares for failing to heed your own advice. Am I right?"

"Hey! I just woke up and my mind's still full of mush," retorted Stella. "How does a girl get some beauty sleep around here, anyway?"

Mac's reply was to throw her pillow at Stella resulting in a furious two-girl pillow fight that echoed down the dorm's corridor and brought several more participants to the fray. The impromptu confrontation was brought to a shrieking halt when Larindo kwark, the seven-foot, eight-inch, 412-pound Sharlee decided she wanted to participate. Nobody wanted the inevitable bruises and/or broken bones that usually resulted from the overexuberant roughhousing for which Sharlees were noted.

One other oddity Sharlees were known for was that they didn't capitalize their family name, but did so with their given name, considering it the more significant.

"Well, I'm certainly awake now," thought Mac. She began thinking about a conversation she'd had some six months ago with her mentor, Professor Yargh, a Dolmrun from Gleb and a highly respected intellect on fusion-powered propulsion. It was a relatively new form of propulsion that had only been made safe for less volatile applications twenty-two years ago.

His explanation of a problem that had vexed the Legion for some time had caused her to make it a personal project from that time forward. She remembered how it had started.

"Professor, I keep hearing about some problem with the multilight speed drive when they are traveling through solar systems like ours that have cooler G or K suns," Mac posed to Professor Yargh.

"That's just it," stated the professor. "All of us who are senior Legion researchers in the propulsion field have yet to get that last kink out of these newish fusion drive systems. Something about the lower solar signature affects the clean 'hit' we should be getting on the atoms. The best way I can describe it is to say that our engines sputter." He shrugged the shoulders of his four arms as if he had no clue.

Mac perked up as she was reminded of an earth similarity. She spoke. "I recall the old tractors on my father's farm having to be tuned up because they had one or more bad spark plugs that kept them from running smoothly. My dad always said, 'Looks like the tractor needs a tune up, it's sputtering.'"

"It's not that easy here," noted the professor. "Our engines don't have spark plugs."

Mac tilted her auburn-crowned head while chewing on her pencil and said, "While that is true, Professor, the principle may be similar."

"How so?" queried Professor Yargh.

Mac explained as though she were tutoring him, "You see, the reason why the plugs were bad was that they had either been made dirty by deposits building up on them or the electrical charge in the space between the metal tips on them was weakened or interrupted due to overuse. Therefore, something about the cooler suns interrupts the fusion process not allowing it to flow smoothly."

"You mean something like a buildup of deposits on a vital function within the fusion drive?" questioned the professor.

"Exactly!" agreed Mac. "We just have to find where that 'buildup' is and figure out how to get it out of there and keep it from coming back every time we come through a G or K star system."

The professor smiled somberly and said, "Though you have brought an interesting scenario to the situation, I'm not certain it will prove to be any more successful than what we have already achieved. But some fresh ideas might help."

"If you need a new perspective to help you solve this problem, I'd be more than happy to assist," stated Mac eagerly.

"I won't say no," said Professor Yargh. "Your fresh outlook might be just the thing we need!"

From that day on, Mac had devoted practically all her free time to trying to solve the issue, but had gotten only so far.

She was still frustrated even six months later. She knew she was missing a vital clue, but she couldn't put her finger on it. It was there, just at the back of her mind, but she couldn't dig it out.

I can't be wasting my time worrying about that right now, she thought to herself. *I have to straighten up this room. It's amazing how messy a room can get after a pillow fight.*

An hour later, as she was leaving the dorm to go to Professor Yargh's lab/classroom, she was confronted by a new frustration. One of her fellow science students approached her with a piece of paper. The student, Chrisy Blackstone, had taken it off the message board in the corridor. As she walked up to Mac, she waved the paper angrily before her.

"They've done it again, Mac!" she shouted. "They have totally ignored your major involvement in the development of that radical new space adhesive and given credit for it to Professor Yargh and his colleagues! It says it right here on this paper. Why are they so adamant in failing to give credit for any accomplishments from us Earth students?"

"I don't know, Chrisy. Why was that notice on the board in the first place?" wondered Mac.

Chrisy blushed as she answered. "I'm sorry," she apologized. "It was a notice about some time trials dealing with the pilot and navigational school. Apparently, the final year students were going through some speed and maneuvering tests to determine their final scores for placement at graduation."

"So how did they turn out?" asked Mac with genuine interest.

"That's just the point!" exclaimed Chrisy. "The team that won had been having some previous problems with their steering. They used some of your brand-new adhesive to repair and tighten the linkage and it proved to be so effective that they won the trials."

"Let me guess," said Mac. "There is no mention of my name as the creator of the adhesive."

"None whatsoever!" returned Chrisy. "Just the part that says . . . um, let me see. Here it is! 'The winning team would like to thank Professor Baylmun Yargh and his associates for the creation and development of the new adhesive, which greatly helped them to achieve their victory.'"

After giving the notice to Mac, Chrisy said her good-byes and left for her first class.

Mac proceeded to march over to building five, go in, turn right down the corridor to the door marked "Physics Classroom and Lab," open it, and walk into Professor Yargh's office. She gave him no time to greet her before saying "With all due respect, Professor, why did you take all of the credit for my discovery of the new adhesive? I just learned about it from an announcement posted on the information board outside the office in my dorm!"

"Oh my," lamented the professor. "That wasn't supposed to come out for another five days. I was planning on telling you the whole story this evening after our labs were completed. I didn't want you to be blindsided by it, but it looks like it happened anyway."

Mac was still hurt and bewildered by her mentor's seeming deception, but said, "It's nice that you wanted to tell me beforehand, but that doesn't change the fact that you took credit for *my* discovery."

Professor Yargh leaned forward in his chair and looked Mac right in the eye and said emphatically, "You must believe me, my dear McCardle. I did not, nor would I ever, try to take credit away from you. I was approached by the judges conducting those time and maneuvering tests along with certain members of the Galactic Legion's Planning Council to ask me how I had come up with the formula for the new adhesive. When I told them that you had been the one responsible for it and that I and one or two of my colleagues had contributed only a few suggestions, they were extremely upset. They said it was unthinkable to have an earthling named as the developer of such a significant discovery, and especially if the earthling was just a fifteen-year-old student. I told them that, regardless of how they felt, a student of fifteen had been the one to do so. Then I asked them if their failure to give you credit was due to the prejudice that was being promoted by many toward the earth and its contribution for acceptance into the Galactic Legion."

Mac was softening in her anger toward the professor and was becoming intrigued by his explanation. She asked, "What was their explanation to your accusation of their motive?"

"They became angry, of course," said the professor. "They insisted that the earth's contribution should never have been accepted because it 'in no way enhanced the advancement of the Legion due to its frivolous nature.'" The professor continued to quote his visitors, "'Where is the serious science or technology in contributing something called a "Cosmic Shopping Mall" enclosed within a starship that flies throughout the galaxy, allowing people from any given planet to spend their hard-earned money in some gigantic store orbiting said planet? It is just encouraging greed!'" Professor Yargh sighed deeply and explained further.

"The result of their visit was to inform me that they would release the results of the tests involving the pilot and navigator school with full credit given to me despite my protests. When I threatened them with taking it to the highest authorities on Earth and in the Legion, they didn't flinch and said that they would spread a flier all over the earth and throughout the Legion before any legal action could be taken. They added that they had enough support within the Legion's hierarchy as evidenced by those members of the Planning Council that were present there in my office. And what's more, this isn't the first time an achievement by someone from Earth has been credited to an alien race."

Mac looked thoughtful as she recalled, "I have heard rumors to that effect, but I thought they were exaggerated stories or misinformation. Is there really a faction that is dead set against the earth?"

"There is," returned the professor. "But I wasn't certain about it until this incident involving your adhesive."

"So, I won't get any credit for the adhesive then," stated Mac as she brought her fist down hard on her desk in anger. She sighed and said, "I'm sorry, Professor, my anger doesn't stem from a desire for fame, it's just that when you work hard on something, you do appreciate a little recognition."

Professor Yargh put his hands gently on her shoulders, and with a calming smile, told Mac, "I perfectly understand. You might like to know that I didn't let my visitors get off that easily. I told them that if they were so adamant against giving you any credit, I didn't care how difficult it would be or how much my reputation would be tarnished, I would do everything in my power to fight them and get your name out there. We finally reached a compromise that named you as a contributor to the project. That should have appeared on that flier you have."

Mac unfolded the paper on which the flier was printed and looked closely at the small print at the bottom. She made a sound of disgust that was accompanied by a similar gesture and said, "Well, here it is in fine print under a list of twelve contributors. I wouldn't be surprised if the janitor who cleans your lab is on this list."

After the professor had a look, he said, "I'll have a talk with the printer and have them enlarge that list, and if I can't get you first on the list, I'll be sure to have your name among the first six and in a somewhat larger font than the other six." He added, "And if I get any feedback from our friends from my committee of visitors, I have some favors I can call in from one or two on the planning council."

"I guess that's the best I can hope for, and I thank you, Professor. I'm really glad my anger toward you was unwarranted, and I apologize for jumping to the wrong conclusion," said Mac with sincere feeling.

The professor smiled appreciatively and said, "My dear, it was perfectly understandable that you would have felt that way after receiving the news in such an abrupt manner. I am just glad that you do trust me enough to accept my explanation. I think that, after this morning's revelations, you are deserving of a day off. I know you have been wanting to do some more work in your small garden behind your dorm."

Mac smiled broadly as she thought about her garden. Her voice sounded calm as she spoke. "Thank you, Professor. That is a wonderful suggestion and I think I'll take you up on it. Every time I work my little plot of ground, I'm transported back home. It relaxes me and that's just what I need right now."

After taking her leave from the professor, but before she could get to her garden, she ran into her roommate, Stella. She and Larindo kwark were headed back to the dorm following an arduous test concerning the thirty-four different ways an insect called a Gronchuratt could infest and destroy the Lum Lum tree from Dimidium in the Pegasus star system.

"Really! Thirty-four different ways?" asked Mac incredulously. "Does that mean that there are thirty-four different ways to prevent it?"

Stella and Larindo both shook their heads simultaneously while saying "Nope!"

Stella added to their direct answer by explaining. "It seems that there are only three ways to combat infestation of the Lum Lum tree by the Gronchuratt, and they are effective on merely five different ones."

"What about the other twenty-nine?" questioned Mac.

Larindo shrugged her massive shoulders and stated, "Then no Lum Lum tree."

Mac giggled along with the other two and said, "I am headed over to my garden behind our dorm, and I'm glad that I only have to deal with flowers and plants from Earth. It's tough enough to only have to deal with a couple of insect infestations. I have no desire to deal with thirty-four."

"Before you do that," said Stella, "would you like to join us for a bite of lunch? We were just going to the Campus Café after we stop at the dorm, but we'd welcome your company and conversation."

"I think I will. I've got something I'd like to run past you two," stated Mac in an ominous tone.

The café was alive with activity due to it being the noon hour, and the three coeds had to wait for twenty minutes to get seated. They were led to a smallish table in a corner away from the bulk of the boisterous crowd.

"Perfect!" exclaimed Mac. "It's as secluded as I could hope for. And even though we'll have to practically shout to be heard—there is so much noise in here—I doubt if anyone will be able to hear, let alone make out what we are saying."

"I'm not sure we will be able to hear what's being said either," remarked Larindo.

Despite the acoustical problem, Mac was able to talk with the other two about her lack of credit for the adhesive.

She had just finished telling them about Professor Yargh's visit from the Legion officials, when Stella spoke up.

"I've heard all those stories about people from Earth who had done something noteworthy being discredited or snubbed by enough officials from the Legion to discourage many of us from even trying to do research outside of our normal studies."

Larindo kwark spoke next. "A lot of the inhabitants of the older member planets in the Legion are especially vocal about their opposition to the earth being considered for membership in the Legion. They are upset that the contribution of an outer-space shopping mall goes against all previous contributions, such as those made by their planets. Even my home planet, Luyten b, whose main inhabitants are Sharlees and not exactly high on the serious, scientific side, has been somewhat critical of Earth's contribution."

"Why are they complaining? Our contribution is unique and exciting!" exclaimed Mac.

Stella answered, "Come on, Mac. You know as well as I do why all those stuffy scientists and bureaucrats are belittling the *Cosmic Mall* contribution." She attempted to mimic the sound of Earth's critics, saying "It's not serious enough."

She was referring to the requirement made by the Legion for any planet they invited to make a contribution in order to be admitted as a member planet.

The Legion had been observing the earth for nearly a century. Their technology was advanced to the point that their scrutiny could not be detected. They had also made visits to the planet for further investigation.

When the governments of the earth had finally realized that they couldn't accomplish successful space exploration without global unity, the Legion had revealed themselves and offered membership to the earth.

That opened up to the planet all of the technological advances in government, science, and especially space travel that the Legion possessed. All they required from the new planet was some kind of nonmonetary contribution that would enhance the quality of life for any number of Legion members.

Before the earth's contribution of the mall starship, the previous ones had been of a serious political, scientific, or educational nature. A social contribution had never even been considered.

It had generally been felt that social systems, and the behavior they generated, were unique to each planet and didn't need to be interfered with.

Larindo responded to Stella's last comment, saying "Personally, I think the Legion has too many stuffy bureaucrats in charge. When I learned about the earth's contribution being accepted, I jumped at the chance at coming to Earth and studying. I figured it had to be a whole lot of fun!"

"I'm afraid the criticism and bureaucratic endeavors will lead to violence against us," stated Mac as she nervously stirred her tea. She came out of her musings, looked at Larindo, and said with surprise, "So you do have a serious side! I've always thought of Sharlees as less concerned with such issues."

"Oh. There are many sides to our fun-loving Sharlee," declared Stella with a wink. "She is one of the most studious pupils in our class."

Mac smiled as she took Larindo's hand, which dwarfed her own, and gave it a squeeze. She noted, "I'm going to start spending more time with you. Hey!" she suddenly exclaimed. "Why don't you two budding horticulturalists accompany me to my little garden and teach me a few things?"

"That would be great, but we have a class at two on

how to rotate wildflowers on a hillside by means of terracing," stated Stella.

Mac returned with, "That's all right. It's amazing how much time I can spend on a one-quarter-acre plot of ground. If you're free by four, I'm certain to still be there for a couple more hours."

"Then it's a date!" confirmed Stella Steel, getting an enthusiastic nod from Larindo.

Professor Yargh was in deep thought as his conversation with Mac was playing out in his mind. *Should I have told her everything about that incident with the officials from the Legion Planning Council?* he wondered to himself. *Their threats were more than just using their influence to keep anyone from Earth receiving recognition for their achievements. They made lightly veiled threats about an organized movement to undermine the "Mall" project.*

He began to think even more deeply about who he could trust with enough authority to investigate their threats and put a stop to them. All of a sudden, he realized who he could speak to and how he would do it.

"I believe those two individuals have more influence than any half dozen Planning Council members."

As Mac got back to her dorm and changed into her gardening clothes, she stopped for the hundredth time to look at the video picture in the five-by-seven frame on her desk. She smiled for the hundredth time as she sat down on the chair to gaze intently on the family scene.

Her father, Sean Stinson, her mother, Evelyn, and a red-headed rosy cheeked three-year-old, McCardle Stinson, stared out at her. The picture was taken at the family farm with the barn and one or two of their Charolais cows in the background.

"Little Mac," as they called her then, was sitting on her father's shoulder, laughing unabashedly as he bounced her up and down. Her mother was encouraging her by turning to face Mac and clapping gleefully. Sean looked every bit the proud father as he carefully held onto his daughter and smiled fully at her enjoyment.

That picture always made her both melancholy and happy. Melancholy, because she missed her home so much. And happy to have had such a wonderful childhood.

"Well, time's a-wasting, as Dad would say. Them crops ain't gonna prosper without my tender touch," she spoke out loud, echoing her father's expression.

Chapter 2

Down On The Farm

The generous gift of a one-quarter-acre plot of land for Mac's garden was on the stipulation that she would recruit two or more underclassmen to maintain the garden and expand it so that it would cover the entire acre that made up the lawn behind her dorm in years to come.

For her efforts, the area would come to be known as "The Stinson Gardens."

As Mac approached her garden, she noted that some of the boxwoods on the border needed trimming. The spring perennials were in full bloom. The tulips, daffodils, and crocuses were all in their glory. The Asiatic lilies over on the inside border would start to bloom in less than a month. As the spring gave way to summer, there would be daylilies, lavender, Russian sage, and butterfly bushes along with all the others. The metal arches on either side of the garden would have beautiful pastel roses covering one and a stunning variegated clematis on the other. The grape arbor along the back of the flower garden would provide shade during the hot summer. Beyond that, the vegetable garden would grow. Mac wouldn't be able to enjoy all of that, though, as she was graduating at the end of spring. Lori Ingram and Sarah Gordon would be taking over.

To the left of the grape arbor was Mac's work area, equipped with a potting bench, a sink with running water, a storage compartment for her tools, and a mini greenhouse. She started to get some pots out of the storage compartment along with the tools she would need, but, as frequently occurred, her mind went back to her days on the family farm.

It was a mid-April morning in 2213 when her father, Sean, had stopped her as she came in from doing the regular chores of feeding the cows and chickens. There had been a soft, thoughtful smile on his rugged face when he put his arm tenderly around her shoulder and sat her down at the big kitchen farm table.

"Mac," he said, "I know you're torn right now. It's hard for an adult to have to make the kind of decision you're facing, let alone an eleven-year-old. I know you love this farm and all the stock you so eagerly care for. To you, it's not a matter of doing your chores; it's a labor of love. I wouldn't even think of asking you to consider making this choice if I wasn't certain of your success if you accept the Legion's amazing offer. You know that very few Earth youngsters have been invited to attend the advanced schools that the Legion has established here. A lot of the students are from alien races and want to study Earth sciences and learn more about our solar system. To be asked to expand your knowledge in this remarkable way acknowledges your unusual intelligence and ability to take in more. It's an opportunity of a lifetime."

"I know, Dad," replied Mac, "but I feel so much a part of the history of our family on this land. Twelve generations of the McCardle family in the North American continent, nine of those generations on this one piece of land in Marshall County, West Virginia. How the family scratched out a living on ninety-four acres of hilly, rocky terrain cut through with narrow stream beds in ravines where you had to pipe sunshine in for a couple hours a day just to be able to see what was in them."

"Wow," injected her father, "I didn't know you had memorized that speech of mine so well!"

"I not only memorized it, Dad, I've become proud of it," Mac said with deep emotion. She continued, "You even christened me with the family name and, while I wasn't happy with it at first, I've grown to feel honored to bear it. When you volunteered to give up all the high-tech farm machinery and advanced agricultural methods to have a part in the 'Back to Basics' farming movement, I thought you were crazy. Why give up all that labor-saving technology and go back to the dirty, sweaty, back-breaking work of three hundred years ago?"

With a nostalgic look in his eye, Sean Stinson said, "My father had gotten so far away from the history of this farm and our family's place in it that when I first heard about the 'Back to Basics' movement and started delving into the family background, I was overcome with a sense of loss. Loss of a family heritage and lifestyle. I felt a need to try and recapture that heritage by convincing my father to try this basic farming style. But he wouldn't hear of it.

"Then when he died in 2204 while working with that

high-tech machinery, I fought with myself for five years over, turning my back on what he believed in, or disrespecting the family heritage. In the end, I realized that you don't follow a course simply because it's the custom, but that you try your hardest to make the most of what's been given to you. What my father had given me in his will was this land, and he knew how I wanted to farm it. Therefore, I was free to farm in whatever way I decided."

Mac continued the conversation, "That's what I've come to appreciate about your decision. When I started helping you and Mom with the work of running a farm the way people did all those years ago, I started to see how using your hands to work the land and tend the stock was so fulfilling, even though it was very hard work. It made you feel a part of the land. That it is yours and something to be cherished and protected. And to think that was only four years ago. But now, when I'm just beginning to see myself working this farm with you and Mom as my path in life, I'm confronted with a choice that will take me far from here and my family. It's not fair!"

A soft voice came from the adjoining room. "A lot of life is about making choices that aren't fair."

Mac's mother, Evelyn, stepped into the room. With light brown hair and laugh lines around her soft, full lips, she looked almost too fragile to be the wife who helped her husband run a "Back to Basics" farmstead.

She contrasted greatly to Sean's six-foot stature, topped by an unruly mop of sandy hair, vivid green eyes, bushy sideburns, and matching mustache.

Together, they had produced two children Mac and her younger brother, Cory, who had recently turned seven and was just old enough to handle some of the minor chores around the farm. He was an energetic little boy who had a knack for causing chaos. He matched his mother in hair color and blue eyes, his father in ruggedness, and his sister in cleverness.

Evelyn said, "If all the choices we had to make were easy and fair, there wouldn't be much challenge to life. We'd also stagnate mentally if there were no challenges to face. Of course, we don't want a life filled with difficult or unfair choices, but when we do have to face them, they can stimulate our thought processes and help us to become mature adults."

She leaned forward and said, "My love, you have already demonstrated a tremendous amount of maturity for one so young and that, coupled with your gifted intelligence, has made your father and I so proud of you! We would never want to hold you back from achieving whatever those qualities can bring to you." She gently moved her right hand through Mac's light red hair and down the side of her face, resting it softly on her shoulder as she continued to look into the now moist eyes of her daughter.

Mac rubbed her eyes, leaned forward, and embraced her mother, saying "I feel so loved that you and Dad never tried to stop me from pursuing advanced schooling. With all the work to be done at home and your views about cutting-edge technology, especially since the Legion arrived, you've never once discouraged me. You're letting me be me. That makes the decision process a little easier."

As Mac sat back up in her chair, her father stood up and walked behind her, leaning over and resting his hands lightly on her shoulders. He kissed her on the top of her head and said, "Honey, I may have opted for the low-tech life, but when I see and hear how you have excelled in your education, I feel nothing but pride. The fact that you enjoy the hard work on this farm as well lets me know that all those brains you have haven't gone to your head."

Mac and her mother suddenly looked at each other quizzically, then at Sean, who comically crossed his eyes, pointed to his head and said, "Duh!" There was a second or two of silence, then all three exploded in laughter.

Finally, Mac softly shook her head as if to clear it of all the clutter from her current dilemma. She looked up, and, with tears running down her face, said, "I hope they'll let me choose a small plot of land to farm at the Galactic School of Science and Technology."

With tears in all their eyes, the three of them embraced each other in a quiet hug.

"I hope you're not gonna do all that icky stuff much longer. I'm hungry!" said Cory as he entered the room with his hands on his hips and a glare on his face.

With that last thought, Mac brought her mind back to the present. She had only a few weeks to come up with an answer to the propulsion enigma before she graduated and left for her training assignment on a Legion star cruiser. If she couldn't come up with it by then, others would have to.

She truly appreciated the privilege she had received by being asked to attend the advanced educational training at this Legion sponsored school. That invitation was only offered to the most promising intellects on the planet. She was, indeed, a child prodigy. But learning brand new forms of alien physics, engineering, and astronomy, in addition to the most advanced forms of Earth science, had been a real challenge.

I'm going to give it one final push to see if I can come up with a solution and then I'll have to buckle down and finish my finals experiment and hope for an assignment on the Cosmic Mall *ship,* she thought to herself. *But without a solution to the propulsion problem, that ship won't be able to operate at full capacity!*

It was twenty-three years after the acceptance of the *Cosmic Mall* as Earth's contribution for membership into the Galactic Legion. The construction of the starship was only about two years from completion. A full five years ahead of schedule.

There would follow two years of training on various ships in the Legion's system. This time would also be used to acclimate fledgling space travelers to the conditions that go with prolonged time in outer space.

Then there was the actual posting of officers and crew for the ship and the hiring of management and employees for the mall. Security would also be a high priority.

After a three-day leave, the ones fortunate enough to get an assignment on the *Cosmic Mall* ship would spend several weeks receiving intensive training on the state-of-the-art systems that ship would have. Included during that time would be the addition of retailers and other clients not already under contract to the mall.

In four to five years, Earth and its inhabitants would become full-fledged members of the Galactic Legion when their contribution was launched into space.

As all of this went through her mind, Mac began filling the pots on her table with dark topsoil mixing in her own concoction of fertilizer. She started to go back, again, to the family farm. This time, she was helping her dad till the soil in a field where they would be growing corn to feed the livestock. She recalled looking up to her father on the tractor and saying "I hope those cows appreciate all the hard work we do for them."

"All they've got to do, darling, is eat it, get fat, and bring a pretty penny at market," Sean Stinson replied. "That's enough appreciation for me."

Chapter 3

Grannison & Edward

"I just can't understand why you believe that, with the efforts we've put forth and the skills we've shown, some imaginary prejudice against Earth will keep us from, at least, some kind of senior appointment. After all, Grann, you are said to be the best Earth-born pilot there is, and one of the best in the whole Legion," stated Edward Butler.

His half-brother, Grannison Loche, who had come to Edward's apartment, observed, "Yes, and you're about to graduate with high honors as one of the best trained navigators in the history of the Starship Operations School."

Grannison and Edward were fifteen years apart in age but had always been close. Grannison's father, Michael, had been killed by a marauder band while he was attempting to rescue a fellow pilot who had crash landed.

That sad incident had given twelve-year-old Grannison a deep desire to follow in his father's footsteps and become a pilot.

Some two years later, his mother had remarried Carlson Butler, an executive member of the starship manufacturing firm that built the ship Michael had flown. Edward had been born one year later.

Edward had looked up to Grannison from the moment "Grann" had taken him for a "little trip to the moon" when he was ten.

For his part, Grannison never resented his mother's marriage to Butler or their subsequent son. He felt very happy for her, and he had a strong sense of obligation toward Edward. He had nurtured Edward's desire to qualify for training at a Legion school and had suggested he go for a degree in navigation.

Grannison continued their current dispute. "But your late entry into the school and my 'advanced' age will not give us favorable consideration by the councils when it comes time to make assignments on the Starshjp *Cosmic Mall*! I keep telling you that I've got reliable information that the Legion and Earth councils want youth on that bridge, and any assignment we might receive will be well below that."

At six-foot-four, the broad-shouldered, black-haired Grannison, who also sported a salt-and-pepper goatee, presented an imposing figure when he adamantly stated his case. Despite that, though, he was a gentle man who led by example. With rare exceptions, he used his physical appearance as a form of mock intimidation.

Edward, who was barely six feet tall with a paler complexion, blond hair, and blue eyes and a wiry physique, had had plenty of experience confronting his older half-brother and was not intimidated in the least. He snapped back.

"If you're referring to the so-called conspiracy to undermine our 'contribution' to the Legion, where is the proof? It's just a rumor that has grown out of proportion and assumed a life of its own."

"Huh!" snorted Grannison. "The proof may not be documented in writing, but how do you explain all of the excuses when anyone from Earth achieves anything of significance and it's written off as either a mistake or said to be an outright fraud?" he continued quickly before Edward could make a comeback. "And when someone does actually get some credit for it at all, it's always as a secondary contributor or assistant and not as the primary author and developer. You remember that grad student in '08 who wrote the paper about the new mining technique that uses about a fifth of the energy of any previous method and leaves, virtually, no footprint?"

"I think they found that he had taken ideas from his Lamatian professor and made a few small changes in the time sequence to make it appear like it was his own idea," returned Edward with a smug look.

"That's what the biased press trotted out as an excuse," retorted Grannison. "But I have it on good authority that it was the other way around. The professor stole the idea and made the minor changes, and he got the credit."

"Have you heard the latest?" Grannison queried.

Edward stated with condescension, "Since I don't frequent the rumor mill, I can't say as I have."

"I'll ignore the sarcasm," said his brother and continued. "A young Science and Tech School student of only fifteen came up with the formula for that adhesive you just used to repair the break in the steering linkage on the hover cruiser your team operated for your finals in maneuvering. I seem to recall the high praise you heaped on the remarkable efficiency of that adhesive."

"You are correct that the adhesive was a resounding success and played a major role in my team's victory in those maneuvers." Now Edward moved on quickly so as to prevent his brother's interruption. "But I seem to remember that the fifteen-year-old whiz kid only received contributor status."

Grannison had anticipated Edward's response and was ready, saying "I know Professor Yargh personally and he has assured me that the student deserved all the credit for the discovery, and she was currently helping him and his colleagues in an endeavor far more significant in which her insight was leading them to a positive result. He added that he had been pressured into accepting credit for the adhesive by influential members from certain Legion councils, to which he agreed only after he was able to persuade them to include the student as a contributor."

"You realize that is only one example, and anecdotal evidence does not prove the point," said Edward with a note of certainty.

"There are days when I wish I'd never taken you on that little trip to the moon," said Grannison. In reality, Grannison knew what a turning point that little trip had been in both their lives. He spoke as he recalled that time. "Actually, my little brother, before I took you with me on that recon mission to the moon, I was just your frequent babysitter. Don't get me wrong. I really enjoyed it. It was fun playing with you and watching you grow up. When you turned seven, I started taking you with me, on occasion, when I flew supply runs on Earth." He stopped as he noticed Edward indicating that he wanted to speak. He motioned him to go ahead.

"I, especially, remember that was a lot of fun. I developed my desire for piloting from that point. But you saw that I had a head for numbers and plotting a course, so you 'steered' me toward navigation."

"Ooh!" groaned Grannison. "You certainly didn't develop any skills in humor." He continued, "When you turned ten, I thought you were ready for something bigger, and that's when I asked you to come with me to the moon to check out a report we had on vandalism at one of the moonberry harvesting stations."

Edward stated, "I had never been in space before, and I jumped at the chance of going to the moon. I can't tell you how much that meant to me. You were my famous big brother. You were considered the best pilot on Earth, and I was this frail, blond-haired weakling who was nothing like you. My skills were more suited to intellectual endeavors. I couldn't compete with the physical skills of most of my peers. And, believe me, they never let me forget it.

"Still," Edward further recounted, "I've never resented you, because you always paid attention to me and never made me feel like I wasn't as interesting or important as you. So you were, and still are, my role model."

"I don't think I've ever heard you call me that. Thank you. No achievement I've made or recognition I've received can begin to compare with the honor of being your role model," Grannison gratefully said. He grabbed his brother's hand, shaking it vigorously, and gave him an appreciative nod.

"Well," he said. "I've got some business to attend to, but it shouldn't take very long. I'll come back in about an hour and we can go for a drink and a burger."

After a shower and shave, Edward picked out a new pair of slacks with his favorite shirt. A blue-and-gold striped polo that could be converted into a full button-down oxford to go to dinner with his brother.

He had a good twenty-five minutes before Grann would be back. He sat down in his one plush chair to relax while he waited. His thoughts went back to that day he made the trip to the moon with his brother.

"This is the second time someone has broken into that moonberry harvesting station," said Grann. "The first time, they damaged some of the crop. This time, they focused on the climate control equipment."

Edward asked the classic question every young one utters, "Why do you think they are doing it, Grann?"

"Some of the cultivators think it's the workers from the other harvesting station over on the rim of the Crisium crater. There is a lot of competition between the two, with some high rollers betting on whose berries will be bigger and taste better. But I don't think so," noted Grannison.

Edward followed with a second question. "Who do you think it is?"

"My money's on a gang of renegade pilots called 'The Patriots,'" offered his brother. "They graduated from the Terran Pilot School a little after me. I know one or two of them, and they were always advocates of remaining separate from any unification of Earth nations. They're just a bunch of loose cannons that got together about seven or eight years ago. Most of their interference has come in the form of harassment, but they have gotten more violent of late. I chalk that up to the Legion's appearance. I can't imagine that they would be the least bit happy about the unification the Legion has generated."

The two sat in silence as Grannison brought his newly designed Luna/Earth Speedercraft in for touchdown at the station's landing pad. They were met by the station's commander, Captain Louis Domico.

"Hello, Lieutenant Loche," said the captain following

Grann's salute. "I didn't know it was father/son day." He smiled down at Edward, who extended his hand to shake the captain's.

Grannison Loche chuckled as he, also, took Captain Domico's hand in a hearty shake. He corrected the captain by saying "Actually, Captain, young Edward here is my brother, not my son. I brought him along because he has a keen sense of sight I thought might come in handy for the search we need to conduct."

"There's no denying that another set of eyes would be good," assured the captain.

He led them to a door that seemed to be built into the moon's surface. He pressed a coded combination into the key-pad, pulled out a small retinal reader from his pocket, put it up to his eye, then placed it on the small screen above the key-pad. The door opened, and he said, "Welcome to the station!"

Once inside, he led them down a corridor flanked by doorways into offices, most of them small, but two of them were quite spacious and well-appointed. They had been hewn into a mound in the moon's surface allowing them to have windows that looked out on the lunar landscape. The second of the rooms had a much larger floor-to-ceiling window with a breathtaking view of the earth.

"These last two offices are for the base commander, which is me, and the very last one is for the head re-searcher and chief grower, Dr. Plimpton," announced Captain Domico with lightly veiled jealousy.

As he approached the end of the corridor, Domico opened the double doors that led into the spacious growing area. At first it appeared in order, but a closer look into the far-right corner revealed a scene of destruction.

The small glass structure that had housed the climate control equipment was shattered and the highly sensitive humidifiers, custom-designed air conditioners, and air exchange units had been mutilated.

The captain spoke with much anxiety. "I can't begin to tell you how devastating this damage is to our project. These moonberry plants are very delicate. They require the most precise settings in temperature and humidity. Even one degree off can ruin the leaves which provide the berries much of their nutrients. Have you, Lieutenant Loche, ever had moonberry wine?" asked Captain Domico.

"Only once," answered Grannison. He thought back and a wide smile lit up his face. He said, "The best wine I've ever had. What smoothness, bouquet, and color."

"That is the reaction of nearly everyone who has ever tasted it," returned Domico. "And if the temperature is off by just that one degree, that wine would be among the worst you've ever had! By destroying the climate control system, those vandals ruined this whole crop of moonberries," he continued. "Besides the loss of revenue, we have lost valuable time. It will take nearly a year to salvage what we can of this crop. Not for wine, I might add. Then prepare the soil that needs to sit for three months in order to accept and blend the nutrients we put in. And, finally, six more months to grow before harvesting."

"How much money will be lost all together?" asked Edward, demonstrating a keen grasp of the situation for a ten-year-old.

Captain Domico looked at Edward with an approving smile and said, "Loss of sales, approximately one hundred thousand dollars. Growing a new crop, including labor and materials, at least fifty thousand dollars. What we might get by selling what we salvage, less expenses, perhaps fifteen thousand dollars. Net loss, one hundred and thirty-five thousand dollars!"

"This act of vandalism was no small prank, then," stated Grannison. "This is a crime that makes a statement, saying 'We don't approve of what you are doing, and we are going to make you pay for it.' No," said Grann, "this is no rivalry between two moonberry stations. This is a far more serious game."

Suddenly, Edward, who had started to search through the rubble, shouted, "I think I found something that might help!"

As Grannison and the captain approached Edward, he held up a badge-like piece of tin. Clearly embossed on it was a large "P" in gold and a symbol underneath of a lightning bolt in red.

Grannison took the badge when Edward offered it to him and examined it, turning it over and over in his hand. He looked up and gave it to the captain, saying "That, Captain, is the logo of a group of disgruntled pilots, who call themselves 'The Patriots.' They have now officially moved from the realm of vandals to full-blown terrorists!"

That little piece of evidence, coupled with Grannison's connections among pilots, helped them run The Patriots to ground and bring them to justice.

It also got Grannison promoted to lieutenant commander and second in command on a star cruiser.

Edward's popularity soared, and he was given the honorary rank of ensign. This allowed him to get into the best schools and, at sixteen, graduate from high school with honors and enroll in an advanced Legion school.

His thoughts took on a sadder tone as he mused on what the next several years included.

Instead of completing his four years in pilot school, Edward's father had taken ill with cancer during his junior year. He and his mother had always told him that working too closely with the chemicals used in the propulsion engines his firm made could be dangerous for him.

His mother said she could take care of him, but, after three months, it was clear she couldn't. So, Edward had to step in. Grann wanted to help, but he had a very important job while Edward was still young. Besides, as he told Grann, "He was my father, not yours, so I'll use my off time to help Mom."

After his father died, both he and Grann helped their mother out, but she had been weakened by having taken care of a dying husband and dealing with her own illnesses.

When she had died four years earlier, nine years had passed. Edward was twenty-seven and had two years to finish in pilot school. Grann told him if he used his two years of pilot training and enrolled in navigational school, he could complete it in two more years and graduate with a master's.

He did so and was ready to graduate with that master's and get a posting to the *Cosmic Mall* ship, despite what Grann said.

Edward came back to the present as a knock came on his door. He opened it to find his brother—he had long ago stopped thinking of Grann as his half-brother—standing there with two beer steins in his hands.

"You know, Eddie. We can't go to dinner without getting ourselves prepared for the evening," declared Grann with a wide grin. "Why don't you fill these two steins up with that stout you've got. Then we can proceed to the Blue Planet Pub for their great burgers and a couple mugs of that new Sharlean brew, The Afterburner, to see if it lives up to its name."

Edward commented, "Knowing how much Sharlees love a good time, I'd say The Afterburner will not only live up to its name, but it will probably kick our main engines into light speed. So, let's forgo my stout and take those steins to the pub! We've got serious business to attend to in our ongoing research of alien brewing technology!" The two brothers departed Edward's apartment laughing and slapping each other on the back.

It should be noted that some four hours later, they returned having fully completed their research as evidenced by the fact that they had, somehow, managed to walk the three and a half blocks from the pub to Edward's apartment in a wildly circuitous route that lasted forty minutes.

The evening had been a rousing success.

Chapter 4

Keanyn

"Where is that map of the swamp?" wondered eighteen-year-old and fourth-year student at the Cadet School for Officer Training, Keanyn Mathews. "I thought it was in the breast pocket of these khakis."

Keanyn and his troop of seventeen other final-year cadets were about to participate in the last, and most important, of seven maneuvers to assess their leadership and decision-making skills. It was called "The Swamp Maneuver" by the cadets, and Keanyn had been chosen as their captain.

This was the most important of the seven because it was the longest and most grueling. In addition, it carried the highest point total as applied to their final grade.

This year, 2217, there were four finalists.

The Larms, a brutishly powerful race of gladiatorial warriors from Nord near Proxima Centauri (successfully debunking the theory that no orbiting body within the star's influence could support life).

The Wyndites from Jandrel who were a hyper-graceful, athletic, and extremely swift race due to having an extra ankle bone and a muscle and tendon structure in their calves that permitted them to run at speeds of thirty-five to forty miles per hour.

The Creedos from Volrawn 7, who had a five-year stranglehold as champions of the exercises and, especially, The Swamp Maneuver, made up the third team. They loved to parade their victories around as if they were on display to be admired by everyone. In essence, they were bad winners.

The Creedos have a highly developed sense of smell with the ability to recall any plant or animal previously detected. It is very difficult to track a Creedo. Nine times out of ten, they end up tracking you.

The fourth team to qualify for the maneuver was, of course, the Earth team. This was only the third time they had done so in the twenty-year history of the exercises since the Legion had come to Earth, and they had never won.

Keanyn Mathews was determined to change that statistic.

That's why he found himself on this hot spring morning in southwestern Mississippi ready to assemble his team for The Swamp Maneuver.

The "Swamp" referred to was in the Achafalayan basin in a section called the Albemarl Swamp. A more uninviting piece of real estate was not to be found in the entire state of Mississippi. It was said of the "Alb" "even the gators don't like it, but the food's good." A dense fog covered the mire on most nights, gathering at dusk and staying till dawn.

As he was about to give up his search for the map, he remembered that he had taken it from his breast pocket, looked at it to get it firmly in mind, and put it . . . into his rear pants pocket. He checked, and, sure enough, it was there. Now he wouldn't have to trust his memory.

Not that I don't have a good memory, he thought to himself. *It's just good to have something concrete to refer to,* he reassured himself.

He knew it would be tough to pull off the victory, but he had what he believed was a great plan.

As he left the barracks, he ran into Zach Demopolis, a short, muscular, twenty-year-old Grecian triathlete who had come to cadet school after winning the Gold Leaf Award four years ago at the fourth Legion games. He had been assigned as lieutenant on Keanyn's team.

He addressed Keanyn, "I am totally psyched to finally get the chance to beat those pompous Creedos, man." He was shouldering a backpack made of an extremely tough but super pliable material called Xeldron. A container of water was clipped to the pack and a hunting knife was affixed to a holder on his belt.

He tied a bandana around his head, gave Keanyn a comrade-like nudge, and said, "It looks like you're ready to go to the staging area as well, ah, Captain." He paused, trying to get used to addressing his good friend with that rank, and stated, "Are you sure this plan of yours is gonna work? It seems a bit risky, as I've said before, but I'm behind you all the way. I want to beat those arrogant Creedos as much as you do!"

"Thanks, Zach, I can't ask for more than that," returned Keanyn. "I can't guarantee the plan will work, or that we won't get disqualified for bending the rules a little bit. I'm counting on the nature of gators and the attitude of certain members of the Rules Committee to be able to slide by." Keanyn was so determined to beat the Creedos that he was willing to push the boundaries to make it work.

"You always seem to know some things the rest of us don't, Captain," remarked Zach as he looked quizzically at Keanyn.

Keanyn answered Zach's hidden question with, "I keep my ears to the ground, Lieutenant. After all, that's part of my responsibility as your captain. Staying one step ahead."

He smiled as he put a companionable hand on Zach's shoulder.

"You can keep your secrets for the time being, but," Zach pointed ahead to a group of buildings they were headed for and a group of people standing next to one of them and said, "those folks over there are going to need to know what they are and soon."

The rest of the team was assembled outside the third, in a series of twelve, barracks, and they snapped to attention as the two "officers" approached and stood in front of them.

"Team Earth reporting and ready for duty, sirs," shouted Ross Carter, who had been assigned as sergeant.

Keanyn had taken stock of his charges as he approached. Hand-picked by him as he had observed them during their schooling and field training exercises. His father, a colonel in a special unit of the military during the clean-up operations following the last war for interstellar control, had prepared him to be a good judge of character.

Keanyn was the only child of his father, who had been in his mid-forties when his wife, Monica, had given birth. His father had been killed when he and his officers were ambushed by a sniper from a group of rebels against the Legion. Keanyn was only ten and tried to take care of his ailing mother, who died three years later. From that point on, he had been raised by his aunt Joan, his mother's sister. But it was his father who was the greatest influence on his young son.

One thing his father detected in Keanyn was that he possessed the qualities of a leader. Self-reliance, a passion for seeing things through to the end, and a brashness that, while having the potential for getting him in trouble, would also exude the confidence that others would want to follow. All of these had contributed to his being selected as captain of the Earth Cadet Team.

One of the female cadets asked how Keanyn planned on beating the Creedos. His answer was, "As you and the rest know, Louise, the Creedos have that great sense of smell and if they have already detected your odor, they can either avoid you when you approach them or lie in wait to ambush you. If they want to toy with you, they will track you for a while before capturing you.

"That is why, since they have been allowed back in the Swamp Maneuver, they have won it five years in a row. The judges decided that that sense of smell gave the Creedos an unfair advantage and exempted them from the maneuver, allotting them a set number of points depending on where they were placed in the contest at the time."

Everyone was nodding their heads as they recalled the situation. Keanyn continued to speak, "Then it was discovered that, for some unknown reason, Creedos were deathly afraid of alligators and that the slightest scent of them made them panic in fear. Therefore, they were allowed back in the Swamp Maneuver. And so, friends, I plan to use that fear against them and bring victory to us for the first time!"

Marjorie Littleton, a Brit from Yorkshire said, "Keanyn, I know we've got to address you as 'sir' or 'captain' during the mission, but I just want to say that, regardless of your plan, I'll follow you as a leader anywhere; you are the best mate I've ever had."

Like a lot of English girls, Marjorie was fair-haired and rosy cheeked. She appeared demure, but her five-foot-five-inch athletic frame exuded fitness and strength and she could party with the best. She added a question to her previous statement. "Are you going to give us any details about your plan?"

The rest of them looked intently at Keanyn awaiting his reply. When he spoke, he did so cautiously, looking upward as if deciding how he would proceed.

He stated, "Thank you, Marj. While I do have a complete plan, it is dependent on certain factors that won't come to light until after we begin the mission. If those factors are altered, I do have contingencies to my plan. Therefore, to give you any details now would be premature."

The team members were disappointed by the lack of information but seemed to understand why they would have to wait for the full details. In fact, Ross Carter spoke up and said, "We understand, Captain. If you told us now then had to change everything later, it would just be confusing and harder to implement."

"Good man, Sergeant," stated Keanyn. "Confusion is one thing we can't afford to have if we are to go out there and kick some Creedo bums!"

The group of cadets shouted "Yeah!" and "Let's go!" with confidence as they marched off to what they hoped would be a date with destiny.

As they neared the staging area, Zach leaned over and whispered in Keanyn's ear, "That was certainly a load of horse manure you shoveled on them back there. Just when are you going to reveal this plan of yours to them?"

Keanyn's reply was, "I think I'll reveal it to them in stages as we get to it."

"You mean when it's too late for them to argue with you about it?" countered Zach.

"I prefer saying that I'm telling them on a need-to-know basis," said Keanyn.

"If that's when I think it will be. And by that, I mean the last minute. They will certainly need to know by then," declared Zach, shaking his head.

"You always were good at stating the obvious," noted the captain.

As Zach chuckled and playfully punched Keanyn on his upper arm, Tom Palmer, the hulking six-foot-four former-heavyweight high-school wrestler, came up to them and said, "What's up, Zach? You and the captain making plans for dinner after we stomp those Creedos into the ground?"

Tom's muscular body was enhanced by wholesome good looks and semi-long blond hair reminiscent of his Nordic ancestry. He was from a modest-sized town in Wisconsin, where he had been the heartthrob of many young ladies.

Keanyn replied to Tom's question, "After we win the Swamp Maneuver, I'll take all of you out to dinner, and that includes paying for your massive appetite, Tom."

"Hey! I'm all for that," said Tom. "I hope you have enough money, sir. 'Cause I know how hungry I can get after these exercises."

"Not to worry," replied Keanyn. "My Uncle Mark promised me a thousand-dollar check if we pulled this off, and he doesn't go back on a promise."

Tom's retort to that was, "Well, that will take care of me, but what about the rest of the troop?"

The officers in charge of the judging heard the group's laughter as they approached the staging area.

"Mr. Mathews, do you and your team find something

funny about the exercise in which you are about to engage?" stated General Anthony Beckton, chairman of the Council for Cadet Maneuvers.

"No, sir!" replied Keanyn in a thoroughly chastised tone.

"Good, then perhaps you would like to state in a loud, firm voice how this seventh and final exercise you cadets so lovingly call 'The Swamp Maneuver' is to be conducted and the rules that apply to it," commanded the General.

Of course, everyone already knew how the maneuver worked and the rules to follow, but the general wanted Keanyn to be disciplined for what had appeared to be a lack of serious concern for what they were about to be a part of.

There was another reason General Beckton wanted to put Keanyn through the wringer. He knew him well because he was also the head officer for the cadet school and had many dealings with the brash, young student and knew that if you gave him an inch. Well, you know the rest of it.

Keanyn didn't flinch at having to be ordered to recite the rules like an unruly school child. He stepped up on the platform, approached the microphone, flipped the on switch to activate the PA system, cleared his throat, and started to speak.

"The cadet teams assembled here this evening to test their skills in this final and most difficult seventh exercise represent the best in our class. We must expect the best efforts our teams can muster. The goal of this Swamp Maneuver is to, by the use of passive laser weapons, figuratively 'kill' or 'wound' enough members of an opposing team to disqualify them from further participation. "In order to facilitate the judges' awareness of the current state of any of the teams, multifunctional devices will be attached to each of the participants. These devices will also allow any other member of a given team to be aware of the status of other team members.

Only that specific team will be able to track the position and condition of members of their own team. Teams will not be able to track the progress of any other team but their own because the frequency of each team's devices is different.

"The Judges Panel, consisting of three members of the Rules Committee and three from the Judicial Committee will be the only ones to have access to the status of all teams and their members. In the event of a tie concerning decisions that have to be made, the chairman, General Beckton, will have the deciding vote."

Keanyn continued in this same tone for another fifteen minutes while most stared at him, but their minds were somewhere else.

A few things were pertinent in the information Keanyn recited. Among them were that the teams were not to proceed more than one-half mile into the interior of the swamp.

If anyone did "accidentally" stray beyond the half-mile limit, they must return to the outer rim of the swamp in a reasonably quick time.

The amount of accumulated minor wounds/serious wounds or deaths would determine the ability of any team to continue.

Short regrouping meetings of no more than ten minutes in length were permitted, and they were not to total more than four during the entire exercise.

Keanyn concluded his lecture, as it were, with, "While these are the more pertinent rules for this maneuver, the other applications will have been discussed during pre-op training. Any extremely unusual occurrences during the exercise will be discussed between the participants and the judges, who will determine if the affected members of the team in question or the team as a whole still qualify to participate. If you have no questions for the council members, I invite General Beckton back to the podium."

Before he could get away from the microphone, Keanyn was asked a question by one of the Creedo cadets named Swooth, "Captain Mathews. We heard you've got some secret plan to beat us. Have you lost your mind?"

"Quite possibly, Swooth," said Keanyn. "But at least I have a mind to lose!"

General Beckton swiftly grabbed the mic and settled the crowd down with a stern glare. He scanned his audience as he made his final address to the teams, "As you know, the chairmanship of the Judicial Committee for these maneuvers is held by a senior officer from the forces on the planet on which these contests are held. It has been my privilege to have been the chairperson for the last seven years. I take pride in the fact that, while I might naturally want a team from the Earth to do well in this competition, I have never given any special consideration or advantage to any Earth team. I believe that has been reflected in the fact that no Earth team has ever won this competition. In fact, I have had the deciding vote on, at least, three previous occasions, to disqualify Earth teams from the maneuvers.

"That being said, I am announcing at this time that I am voluntarily relinquishing my chairmanship and participation on the Judicial Committee following the current competition. I have accepted an invitation to become a member of the Legion's Executive Planning Council as its first Earth-born representative."

This announcement was met with immediate cheers and applause by not only fellow council members but the cadets as well. While many of them felt the general to be a strict leader and disciplinarian, they respected him as a fair and honest man in whom they would put their trust in any circumstance.

The general paused to regain his composure. He now spoke in his official capacity as chairperson. "It is now time to commence this final maneuver. Terrain hovercraft will transport each team to their predesignated egress points. These have remained undisclosed to you participants so that no knowledge of the starting point of any team will be known to the others. The transporting order will be as follows: The team with the most points will depart first. That team is the Creedos. The second will be the Wyndites. The Earth team will be third, and the fourth will be the Larms."

The transporting was done in this descending order so that each team with less points would have, at least, a slight advantage in knowing the general direction one or all the other teams would enter the swamp.

The general scanned his gaze over the four teams assembled before him and said, "Ladies and gentlemen of the Cadet Officers School, are you fully prepared for the test of your skills this Swamp Maneuver will present to you?"

Their answer was a strong and affirmative one. They were certain they would come through the night's ordeal the victor. There was no possible way their team would lose.

Reality, of course, would prove otherwise, and many a sad tearful face would greet the dawn at 6:00 a.m.

General Beckton concluded his address with the following encouragement.

"Therefore, cadets, I wish you well, and may you demonstrate proudly how the training you've received here has molded you into the officers you will need to be as you take your place on the starships of the Galactic Legion!" He, then, saluted them in a farewell gesture.

Zach whispered into Keanyn's ear as the members of the Judicial Committee exited the platform. "Did you know the general had been chosen for the Executive Planning Council?"

Keanyn's reply was cryptic. "It certainly did answer some questions I had."

"And what is that supposed to mean?" said Zach, with a perplexed look on his face.

"Tell you later" was Keanyn's evasive reply. He continued, "Right now, I want to see in which direction the Creedos are going. I hope it's toward the west because that will play nicely into my plans."

With that, the first of the hover vehicles arrived and carted the Creedos south . . . then west.

Zach looked over at Keanyn as a playful smile spread across his face and he said to him, "I don't know all the details of your plan, but when I see that ornery smile on your face, I know it means we're in for fun—and trouble!"

Keanyn replied. "We shall see, my friend. We shall see."

Chapter 5

The Swamp Maneuver

Keanyn's troop was transported eastward along the perimeter of the swamp. An unfortunate start in the opposite direction of the Creedos, adding more time and effort to his plan.

There was an advantage to this, as it would give him more time to tweak some of the less-than-certain points in his strategy and to bring the rest of the team up to snuff on his plan. So he explained it to them, with the following response from Ross Carter, "With all due respect, sir. Have you lost your mind?!"

The twenty-one-year-old California-born but New Jersey-raised son of Henry "Butch" Carter, police commissioner of Newark, New Jersey, had an expression of incredulity, and his body was shaking as he barely kept himself under control.

Zach took the opportunity to comment. "I thought you said you were going to tell them gradually to help them get their minds acclimated to your plan. This sounds like the whole ball of wax. And, if you don't mind my saying so, Captain, more than a bit risky."

"'More than a bit risky'?" repeated Ross. "This plan could not only get us disqualified from this maneuver but also force us to forfeit all of our points and jeopardize our graduation. A bit risky? It's insane and dangerous!"

The group took in a collective breath as they wondered if Ross had crossed the line with his comments. As they feared a sharp reprisal from Keanyn, Ross leaned forward with a conspiratorial smile and said, "On the other hand, it sounds like a whole lotta fun, and I wouldn't miss it for the world."

Keanyn grabbed Ross in a bear hug and said, "I wasn't fooled for a minute, Ross. I knew if anyone would be up for this crazy scheme, it would be you."

"I may have a screw loose, sir, but I was finding this whole swamp thing a little boring," responded Ross. "I was hoping you had something up your sleeve to liven things up."

"This will more than liven things up," said Zach, then added, "If we don't pull this thing off just right and follow up with a pretty good explanation to the judges, we could be out of the competition completely."

Keanyn scanned the eyes of his troops to assess their determination and noted what he found by saying "If I read you all correctly, I think I have the support of each and every one of you. Am I right?"

His answer came from seventeen heads all nodding their affirmative in unison.

"What gave you the idea for this plan in the first place, sir?"

questioned Cheng Wong, an eighteen-year-old Chinese girl whose family had been smugglers of exotic oils from India into China. When she and her family had been caught, it was noticed that her skills as a lookout and her incredible quickness and agility had been the reasons it had taken six years of intense effort to finally capture them.

Instead of sentencing one so young to years of incarceration, the Legion decided to use her skills for better purposes. She, and two other family members, were sent to Legion schools to train their former unlawful activities into uses more beneficial to the Legion.

Keanyn's answer filled in some of the gaps he had left from the initial revealing of his plan. "When I found out that we would be facing the Creedos in the Swamp Maneuver, I started thinking about how I could use their fear of gators with their incredible sense of smell in order to turn it into a big enough advantage to defeat them.

"I came up with the idea that, if someone could manage to panic them with the scent of gator, the Creedos would retreat and run into an ambush. That would spell their doom. The question was, where could I find a way to get the scent of gator without actually bringing a live gator along? The answer was put right in my lap, literally."

They had been walking westward for about an hour in a tight group in order to converse so they wouldn't be considered as having one of their four short meeting stops. But at Keanyn's mention of the answer being put in his lap, Zach stopped, thus halting the group, and said to Keanyn, "Do you mean you had a gator put right in your lap?" He was wide-eyed and dubious at the same time.

"Actually," said Keanyn with a look of disgust on his face. "I had gator pee accidentally spilled into my lap by an overexuberant lab student. It seems they had collected several samples of the stuff to test for possible uses as an ingredient in insecticide."

"What did they discover?" asked Tom.

"Not much, Tom. Essentially, they found out that gator pee stinks! But they gave me the answer to getting the scent of gator without the gator. I went back to that lab a few days later and asked if they had any spare gator pee and they gave me four six-ounce vials of it. No questions asked. They said the quicker they got rid of the stuff, the happier they would be."

Everyone laughed quietly, then Tom Palmer remarked, "I would think that cutting through the swamp like you plan will give us plenty of chances to corral a gator," he said.

"True enough, Tom, but I don't think any of us wants to deal with a live gator," returned Keanyn. "Besides, the smell of gator pee will spread their scent a lot faster."

Another cadet named Dooley Paxton, who hailed from Louisiana, spoke up, "I suppose that's why you included me in this little soiree, Captain. Being the son of a Loosiana gator farmer might make the crossing of the swamp a little safer."

"I can't deny, that was a big reason for including you, Cadet Paxton," noted Keanyn. "But you have other skills that can prove to be assets to the team."

"I appreciate that, sir, but when you said we would be going through the swamp to get to something called the 'Creedo Duck Blind,' I began to lick my chops at the prospect of confronting some gators," said Dooley with a satisfied smile.

"That's right!" exclaimed Marjorie. "What is the 'Creedo Duck Blind'?"

Keanyn told them about being out one night at a local club, where he ran into a disgruntled Creedo he had bribed into revealing a special scheme they were using.

"It seems that the Creedo team found and spruced up an old duck blind that had been abandoned several years ago. They use it to ambush other teams. That's the way they've been able to win five years in a row. I figure that by cutting through the swamp, we can get to that duck blind before anyone else. Then we start strategically spreading that gator pee about one-half to three-quarters of a mile before we get to the blind. That should flush out the Creedos, who will run in a panic away from us and into the waiting arms of the rest of our team."

"I see," said Ross. "That's why you said we would separate into two teams. One to go through the swamp and the other to circle round to meet the Creedos."

"Exactly!" declared Keanyn.

Zach had been rubbing his chin in thought while Keanyn had explained his plan and remarked, "Captain, I see a lot of risk in this, and I don't just mean cutting through the swamp and the gators. After we split, what keeps the other half of our team from discovery by the other teams and possible defeat by being outnumbered?"

"I never said there wasn't a good deal of risk involved, but I don't fear too much from the Larms. They generally rely on their brute strength and don't use their minds to calculate strategies. The Wyndites are ultra-athletic and intelligent, and I can see them taking out the Larms fairly quickly. The Creedos will be single-minded in setting up their duck-blind ambush and shouldn't even be a concern. Our main concern is the Wyndites, who entered the swamp before us. So if we proceed for the first three or four hours slower than we usually do, we should stay behind them and I'm hoping that the other part of our team will be able to pull off a surprise ambush from the rear."

Keanyn hesitated before he made his next statement.

"That is why I want you, Zach, to lead that second group. In fact, you will have two-thirds of the group. I am only planning on taking five others with me."

He knew this would elicit a strong remark from his lieutenant, and he wasn't surprised when Zach uttered his protest in an angry but subdued voice. "Captain, I have been by your side in every maneuver during this cadet test. We are a team within a team. And now, during the most important and difficult maneuver of the seven we have faced, you want us to separate! Why?" Zach's face clearly showed the hurt and confusion he felt.

Keanyn walked up to Zach and put his hands on Zach's shoulders and looked into his eyes with the expression of comradeship and said, "My brother. It is for the very reason you cite that I ask you to lead that group. You and I are, indeed, a team within a team. We have worked so closely together in complete cooperation that if I can't lead the team, having you do so is like having me do so!"

Zach looked straight into Keanyn's eyes and saw no flattery. Only sincerity and confidence in him and in his ability to succeed.

He dropped his head, heaved a sigh, and stood at attention, saluting his captain, saying "Yes, sir! Whatever your orders, I am prepared to carry them out, sir!"

"That brings us to the point of coordinating our two teams so that we can pull this off with precision," stated Keanyn.

"Let me guess," said Cheng. "After all, breaking rules was my life for over seven years." She continued, "You make up some story about gators, somehow diverting some of the team into the swamp. Then there has to be some way in which the detection devices of those going into the swamp will be made inoperative. That way the judges won't be able to track you. Am I right so far?"

"Spot on," noted Keanyn. He motioned for her to continue.

"Zach, or— I'm sorry—Lieutenant Demopolis will then act as liaison between us and the judges and to plead our case to get permission to proceed despite the damaged detection devices," she finished and stood at attention as Keanyn replied.

"Very good, Cadet Wong," he commended her. "In a nutshell, that's how I've planned it. Your skills are excellent, and that's why you will be on my part of the team. The other four are cadets Tom Palmer, Louise Munoz, Dooley Paxton, and Sergeant Ross Carter. I am making a field promotion of Marjorie Littleton from cadet to sergeant to assist Lieutenant Demopolis."

Tom Palmer injected an interesting question. "Sir, if you don't mind my asking. If we do encounter gators in our trek across the swamp, we will probably have to use our guns. How can we do that and not give away our position?"

"Very astute question, Cadet Palmer," remarked Keanyn, who smiled and answered. "I had given thought to that problem myself and took the liberty of rigging up silencers for our pistols. And, before you ask, I checked the rules thoroughly and found no stipulation against modifications made to the weapons, just the prohibition against substituting another weapon for the ones we were issued."

Zach, who had been nervously fidgeting while they had been stopped for discussion, spoke up quickly. "Captain, if you don't want to get disqualified for standing still too long, I suggest we keep moving."

"Indeed, Lieutenant. We don't want to get disqualified before we even go two miles into the Albemarl Swamp."

About another two miles along, they came on a very disturbed section of ground, denoting signs of struggle.

"What do you make of it, Captain?" wondered Louise.

Keanyn studied the ground for a few seconds and said, "The two distinct set of footprints suggests two different teams. My guess would be the Larms—note the marks of heavy boots—and the Wyndites—the contrasting lighter tread of their shoes."

"Very good, captain!" stated Dooley enthusiastically. "The eventual overlapping of the lighter steps of the Wyndites tells me that they prevailed and captured the Larms, who they appeared to lead off in that direction." He pointed toward the northwest and the outer rim of the swamp.

"Do you think we should follow to find out what's going on?" questioned Zach. He continued, "We might be able to obtain some valuable information, if we're careful."

"I think that's a good idea, Lieutenant," agreed Keanyn. "But I'll have to contact the judges to get special permission for some of us to make a reconnaissance run while the rest of us wait. And another thing. Does anyone here speak the Larmish tongue, Larmique or Salmeaze, spoken by the Wyndites?"

Peter Dubois, a twenty-year-old French tennis pro, who spoke seventeen Earth languages and had added twelve alien tongues in the last seven years, raised his hand and said, "Most assuredly, *mon captaine,* I am fairly well-versed in those *deux*—" he stopped and corrected himself. "I meant to say two tongues."

Keanyn, who was quite familiar with Peter's linguistic prowess, stated, "Excellent! Why don't you and Cadets Wong and Palmer follow the Wyndite trail and see what you can learn. Don't be any longer than fifteen minutes. I'm sure the patience of the judges won't tolerate more."

"Yes, sir" came the reply of all three.

When they returned twelve minutes later, Tom reported the following: "After going only about one-quarter of a mile, we heard what appeared to be a heated discussion between several Larmian cadets. We couldn't get a good view of them without being seen, but we found a thick group of bushes to hide behind that allowed us to eavesdrop on their conversation. I would guess there were about five of them. According to Peter's interpretation, they had either been 'killed' or seriously 'wounded' by the Wyndites, who had ambushed them, more than enough to render their team disqualified. I'll let Peter give some of the details of their 'colorful' conversation."

Peter flushed as he began his discourse. Apparently, the Larms' anger at being disqualified was quite evident in their speech, but Peter cleaned it up as he went along.

His hazel eyes were wide, and his strong square jaw was set as he began. "They speak as if others are to blame, not themselves! Their misfortune is due to the actions of others instead of their own carelessness and stupidity! *Mon dieu!* What a group of—how you say—strong-headed?"

Zach broke in with the correction. "I think you mean 'hard-headed.'"

"*Mais oui!*" responded Peter. "A most hard-headed people." He coughed nervously as he realized he'd gotten away from the original point. "I apologize for getting off track, as you say. My feelings about the Larms are not important," he said with a bowed head. He continued. "Their conversation seemed to center around the Wyndites being able to take them completely by surprise. They hadn't realized how quiet and—ah, I am thinking of the word." His face lit up as he captured the desired word. "Yes, 'stealthy'! That is it! How stealthy they were. They had, obviously, paid no attention to that fact in the six previous competitions!"

Peter blushed once more and said, "*Excusez-moi*, but once again I divert."

The others hid smiles as they recognized the word Peter wanted to use was "digress."

The Frenchman hurried on. "The Wyndites' initial attack seriously wounded two and killed one Larm. Their captain, Rodux, ordered a retreat toward the perimeter of the swamp, but on their way, they were ambushed by a small group of four Wyndites who killed two and wounded three more Larms, which eliminated them from the competition."

Peter tried to smooth down his full mop of wavy brown hair as he concluded.

"What made them especially angry is that there were only nine Wyndites in the group that attacked them. That means they were defeated by a group at merely half strength! Ooh la la! That is embarrassing, *n'est-ce pas*?" He finished with a chuckle.

"Yes, it most certainly is, Peter," stated Keanyn, who asked the obvious question. "Where were the nine other Wyndites?"

"According to Peter, the answer was given by the Wyndites themselves," declared Cheng Wong. She looked at Peter who gave her a sign to continue. She explained by saying "Since their language has some similarities to Cantonese, I have been studying Salmeaze myself and have been itching for an opportunity to translate it. So, here goes! They felt there would be no harm in divulging certain details of their plan to a defeated group of Larms. After all, they wouldn't be able to pass it on to any other team. They were done for the night and had to leave the swamp as soon as it was confirmed by the judges. The joke was on them, though." She continued to give further details. "Captain Mathews, the Wyndites, or at least their lieutenant, Aeryanee Larmuth, said that their captain, Yarmeul Sensa, seemed to have found the same disgruntled Creedo as you, sir. He also bribed him like you to obtain the info concerning the duck blind scenario."

Everyone looked very concerned at this revelation. Some of them began to wonder if their plan would succeed.

Keanyn looked at Cheng and said, "What did Captain Sensa do with the information?"

"He also determined to split his group, but not cross through the swamp," stated Cheng Wong. She continued, "They split within a few minutes of arriving, with one half led by Captain Sensa heading east around the swamp and the other half going west along the perimeter as well."

"That explains why we didn't run into the one heading west," noted Ross. "By the time we got here, they would have already been by. We arrived at the swamp not much farther west than they did and some fifteen to twenty minutes later."

Keanyn acknowledged Ross' observation as correct but added, "I'm still not clear on their strategy for splitting up, unless they planned to box the Creedos in their duck blind."

Cheng looked at Keanyn and winked her eye while giving him a thumbs up. She said, "That's exactly right, sir. Once they eliminated the Larms, which was a last-minute adjustment, they would only have to worry about us, and with their speed and agility, they could keep well ahead of us and make a beeline for the duck blind."

"But we now have the advantage. Because we know their plan and we can negate a lot of their speed when we cut through the swamp," declared Keanyn with a smile on his face.

Zach took a different angle, having his group in mind. "That is all well and good, Captain. Except you've left out my group. How does this knowledge affect us?"

"It actually improves your situation," returned Keanyn. "The Wyndites will be staying way ahead of you but will need to slow down as they approach the Creedos' position. You can catch up with them, especially if we have arrived and caught the other half of their team by surprise. Lieutenant Larmuth's group wouldn't advance, having to go right by the Creedos to do so."

"I see," said Zach. "Then we can ambush the other half of their team from behind. Things are beginning to look up!" he added with a broad grin.

Keanyn had an urgent look on his face as his mobile comm unit vibrated. "If I'm not mistaken, that's the judges panel telling me we've got to go. So, let's move out!"

After they had gone another mile and a half, following the edge of the swamp in a southeasterly direction, they were halted by Keanyn. He looked up from his map, checked his compass, and said, "We have arrived at the point where the six of us will break off and enter the swamp. In a few minutes, Zach will radio to the judges' panel that several alligators have aggressively encountered our group and caused the six to become separated and head into the swamp to avoid them.

"In the meantime, our group will take our homing/status devices off and beat them around a bit as if we are in a struggle with the gators. It will be vital that those devices get so abused and doused in the swamp waters that they become inoperative.

"During all of this, I will be trying to desperately keep in contact with the judges. Unfortunately, my comm unit will suffer the same fate as our homing devices, and Zach will take over the communications from there."

Zach was shaking his head while smiling broadly. He looked at Keanyn and said, "In the four years I've known you, Captain, I've never heard you utter such a load of crap as you have just done. Do you really think that will convince the judges?"

"Didn't you and I take a little six-week acting class last summer? I told you then we might have to incorporate some acting skills at some point in our training," he explained further. "Now's the time to put that training to work! It is a risk, but if we do it right, we have a good chance of getting away with it."

Zach was still a bit doubtful but said, "I've followed a number of your crazy schemes before and they always seemed to work out. I guess I'll do it again."

"That's the spirit!" declared Keanyn. "Now, let's get started."

In under fifteen minutes, they had accomplished the damaging of the homing devices as well as rendering Keanyn's comm device unusable and had advanced some five hundred yards into the swamp.

Now came the most critical part of the plan: convincing the panel of judges to accept the less-than-accurate account of their situation.

"I'm certain that none of the six have been seriously injured, General," reported Lieutenant Demopolis to General Beckton, chairman of the judges' panel.

"How many gators were there, Lieutenant?" asked the general.

Zach's reply was edged with nervous anxiety, which he did not have to pretend. "It all happened so quick, sir, that I couldn't get an exact count. But I'd say at least four of them. They just came up out of the swamp onto the path we were on near the border. There was a gap of about ten yards or so between our part of the team and theirs, and the gators came in there and cut off our two groups."

The general sounded less than convinced as he stated, "It appears that all of their homing/status devices have malfunctioned, and Captain Mathews' comm unit is inoperative as well. Is that correct, Lieutenant?"

"To my knowledge. Yes, sir!" Zach was reluctant to sound completely convinced. After all. He was lying to a superior officer.

"One final question, Lieutenant. How far into the swamp do you estimate Captain Mathews and his group were forced?" General Beckton emphasized the word "forced" as if he was less than convinced.

Zach took a deep but silent breath as he answered the doubting general. "By way of Captain Mathews' own estimate, I would say at least one-quarter of a mile, sir. And, per the captain's last communication, they were being driven toward the one-half mile limit, and probably beyond."

It was nearly a minute before the general responded. When he did, his words did not fill Zach with confidence. "I and my fellow judges will now consider your situation, Lieutenant. I'm certain there will be many questions they will want to consider. I estimate that it will take us some fifteen to twenty minutes to arrive at a decision. In the meantime, I suggest you make whatever efforts you can to try and establish communication with Captain Mathews and prepare for either continuation or disqualification of your team in the Swamp Maneuver."

In fact, it was twenty-five minutes later before Zach received the panel's decision.

General Beckton spoke firmly and clearly as he said, "Lieutenant Demopolis, the panel has thoroughly discussed your situation, and our decision was not arrived at without controversy."

That statement did not instill any confidence in Zach's hopes for a positive resolution. But he did not show it outwardly as the General continued. "While many of us would not put it past Captain Mathews to fabricate this incident in order to gain an unfair advantage by making it look like an unavoidable accident that he and others from your team had to go deep into the swamp, there are those who feel that if we decided to disqualify you without solid proof, we would do you an injustice. Especially if it came to light that your story is accurate."

Now Zach wasn't sure how to feel, but it did seem to sound a little more in their favor. General Beckton paused before announcing their decision.

"Therefore, the panel has decided that you may continue under the stipulation that you attempt to rendezvous with the rest of your group ASAP! Also, those six members who are within the interior of the swamp are considered as having sustained minor injuries. One final detail. You, Lieutenant Demopolis, are now promoted to acting captain. You may make a second-in-command of your choice. Is that understood, Captain?"

"Yes, sir!" was the greatly relieved reply of Cadet Captain Zachory Demopolis.

When he reported the panel's decision to the rest of the team, they all responded with a thumbs up. Zach began to lay out their course from that point forward. Their attention could now be given solely to catching up to and dealing with the Wyndites.

"They have probably started slowing their progress as they neared the Creedos' duck blind," he noted. "My guess is that we are within one-half mile of their position."

He was thinking on the run and trying to recall Keanyn's methods in similar situations.

Come on, Zach, he thought to himself. *What have you learned in all the time you've spent with that cunning son of a gun?*

When he had finished ruminating, he moved quickly into a plan of action.

"Sergeant Littleton. Take half of the team and move forward one-quarter mile, fanning out on either side of the path in whatever cover you can find. The rest of us will move at a slightly slower pace to the same point and block the path to prevent either a Wyndite retreat or a more panicked Creedo one. In either case, we should be able to halt and outflank our adversaries and eliminate them from this maneuver."

Peter Duboise voiced a concern on the minds of several team members. "Captain, how are you so certain that one or both of those teams will be retreating?"

"Excellent question, Peter," stated Zach. "The rest of you don't know Keanyn like I do. When he says he is confident of his plan succeeding, then I am as well. In fact, from the moment we received permission to move forward once we were separated, I had no doubt about the success of our endeavor! Therefore, if Captain Mathews says that we will defeat the Creedos, then WE WILL defeat the Creedos! And that means they will be in retreat from what they perceive as an attack of gators, and if the Wyndites happen to get in the way, they will end up retreating as well."

The loyalty and trust in their captain that Zach had just exhibited was a catalyst for the rest of them to do the same.

Marjorie Littleton proudly spoke. "Captain Demopolis, when I said earlier that Keanyn was the best mate I ever had, that is now true ten times over!"

In the meantime, the six cadets led by Keanyn were plodding through swamp water up to their hips as they kept a wary eye on those waters for any sign of gators. Most of them were not skilled in detecting the subtle movements of a gator if one was indeed tracking them.

Fortunately, Dooley was an expert at noticing any slight change in condition and knowing how to handle it. It was for that reason that he had dropped quietly out of the lead position and made his way stealthily toward the rear of the line where Keanyn was positioned.

He had noticed an ever-so-tiny ripple in the water coming from a bank of cypress to their west. He had also taken note that the wind had shifted and was coming from the east, putting them upwind of that cypress bank. One of those factors might mean nothing. Two of them together spelled trouble in Dooley's experience.

As he neared Kenyan's position, the captain looked quizzically at Dooley and tilted his head as if to say, "Is there a problem?" Dooley's answer was a shrug of his shoulders and a quick, "It may be nothing, but it could be a gator. Just checking."

Dooley had seen what he had feared. Two round eyes just above the surface of the water, not more than thirty feet behind Keanyn, and they looked to be focused squarely on the captain. An attack was imminent, and Dooley had to act quickly and decisively.

He dove under the water just as he got past Keanyn. The gator made its move, almost simultaneously, in a lunge that brought it halfway out of the water as it leaped for the startled captain!

Halfway through its lunge, Dooley burst out of the water, brandishing an eighteen-inch-long hunting knife with a twelve-inch blade. He tackled the ten-foot gator with his left arm while positioning the knife in his right hand. Both combatants disappeared under the water as they churned up a tempest on its surface.

The rest of the team stood frozen in place for a good ten seconds before Keanyn and Ross moved forward to see if they could give Dooley any help. Their inability to see who was who or what was what made any attempt to provide aid impossible.

As the water continued to churn in its cauldron-like upheaval, the two contenders would occasionally surface, locked in a combat to the death. During the fourth such occurrence, they noticed Dooley's right arm making quick thrusting motions. Then the gator wrapped its claws around Dooley's knife-wielding arm, forcing the gator hunter to drop the knife, which he deftly caught in his left hand.

Then they saw Dooley make a slashing motion with his left arm, followed by a complete stillness in the water, and then total silence.

After several seconds, the water rippled again, and a hulking form began to emerge. Everyone stood in fearful anticipation awaiting the identity of the probable victor.

The emerging form turned into Dooley Paxton, whose blood-stained arms and torso wavered for a few seconds before he took a step or two and fell face down into the water.

Keanyn and Ross quickly dove in and recovered his still-breathing body and carried him toward higher and drier ground.

Cheng retrieved articles from her first-aid kit, looked dejectedly at the inadequate medical supplies, and held back a sob as she knew it wouldn't be enough to save Dooley's life.

The Wyndite second-in-command, Larmuth, was instructing his group of nine on the need to fan out across the path to form a makeshift wall as they advanced on the Creedo duck blind in order to force them into defending themselves on two fronts. As long as they remained downwind of the Creedos, their presence would go undetected and provide the element of surprise that they hoped would give them the advantage they needed in order to take out those pompous braggarts.

The need for a rear lookout was suggested by one of the cadets, and Larmuth appointed Cealdan, a particularly agile and observant member of the team to patrol their rear some one hundred yards back.

That nearly proved the undoing of Zach's team as they came within the one-quarter-mile limit he had decided would be a safe distance from the Wyndites.

Cealdan perked his ears up, thinking he heard rustling sounds not too far behind. Before he radioed back to Larmuth, he decided to investigate more closely to make certain it was no false alarm. That delay saved Zach's team from being discovered.

Here is where Jonas Alexander Philpot proved his worth in being selected as part of the Earth team. Jonas, or JA, had been the odd man out in the otherwise athletic, muscle-bound, or agile members of Keanyn's team.

He was short, just a little clumsy, and possessed no athletic skills beyond chess or other cerebral board games.

His mind was always busy figuring out chess strategies or mathematical equations. His wildly tousled brown hair and thick glasses sitting atop a pug nose made him look anything but a member of a guerrilla-like company of cadets on a military mission.

A few minutes earlier, Jonas had questioned Zach on

the need for a scout to go ahead and make sure "the coast was clear."

"Don't you think the Wyndites are concentrating on the Creedos, who are ahead of them, Cadet Philpot?" asked Zach.

JA's reply was "I have this gut feeling that they would send a lookout to make sure we are not behind them." He paused before bringing up more of Keanyn's advice. "You know what Captain Mathews says about gut feelings?"

"All too well, JA, all too well." Zach now paused, recalling Keanyn's exact words. He then began quoting his close friend. "'My father told me that if you had a gut feeling so strong, no matter how ridiculous it might seem, go with it! He said that it had proved true with him on at least three occasions.'"

JA spoke, "He told me he had the same gut feeling about me being on his team. Well, here I am, and now might just be the time when his gut feeling will pay off with mine, sir."

Zach hesitated, considering if it was wise to make a decision based on not one but two gut feelings. He finally made his decision and told JA.

"Cadet Philpot, you may proceed to move ahead of the team some one hundred yards in order to determine if the Wyndites have posted a rear guard. You must accomplish this using all the skills you possess. Including stealth and agility along with keen eyesight and hearing."

After saying that, he was having doubts about sending JA on this assignment.

JA responded with, "I'm not sure I have much skill in those areas, Lieutenant. But you can count on me to give it my all, sir!"

That's why Jonas found himself hunkered down in the vegetation of a hammock in the path of an advancing Cealdan, hoping he wouldn't make a complete fool of himself and jeopardize the success of the mission in the process.

Cealdan was getting closer to JA's hiding place, becoming more and more certain he was detecting the movements of another team. Just a little bit closer and he would be sure.

He came some ten yards closer and caught a glimpse of a human form through the foliage. He was preparing to radio Larmuth with this info when JA sprang into action.

He had to muster up all his courage and try to remember the little training he, a cadet studying communications, had received in hand-to-hand-combat training.

If you don't do this, JA, he said to himself, *no one else will. And then where will the team be? Your failure to act could even jeopardize the success of Keanyn's team. I can't let that happen!* he silently shouted. Then he acted.

He leaped up from the bushes and managed to knock down a totally-surprised Cealdan. He jumped on top of him and held him down.

"Wow! That was easier than I thought!" he said. He rolled Cealdan over in order to secure his hands when he noticed a lumpy, hard, tree root that Cealdan had obviously fallen on.

"That explains why you haven't put up a struggle or cried out," he noted. Then he addressed the fallen Wyndite. "Has that protruding tree root taken your breath?" JA casually asked.

When he received a frantic affirmative nod and noticed Cealdan's normally deep-blue complexion turning a deep red, he sat him up and told him to try some slow deep breathes if he could manage it.

Just then, Marjorie arrived to check on JA and took one look at the scene, stared in disbelief, and knelt down beside the prostrate Wyndite.

"Are you choking?" she calmly inquired. He shook his head "no."

She asked him a second question. "Can you drink some water?"

He managed to whisper an answer. "Perhaps a couple of swallows."

Marjorie gave him the water, and when she made sure he was breathing better, stuffed a gag in his mouth and a bandana around his neck to secure it.

"That wasn't very nice," stated JA. "After all, he was just beginning to get his wind back."

Marjorie looked at JA and said, "He is the enemy right now, JA. I was concerned for his health, but once I ascertained he was all right, I didn't want him calling out to his team or radioing them our position."

"Speaking of radioing, I think his is going off," observed JA.

The rest of the team caught up to them at that point and Zach said, "Good job, Marj. I'm glad I sent you to check on JA."

Marj's reply astonished Zach. "I had nothing to do with his capture. Cadet Philpot did that all on his own. I just gagged the Wyndite so he couldn't warn his team."

Zach and the rest of the team looked at JA in disbelief. Zach said to JA, "When I gave you permission to scout ahead to make sure the Wyndites hadn't sent someone back to check and see if anyone was following them, I did so thinking that there wouldn't be anyone. In fact, I had considered the possibility of them having a rear guard, and dismissed it. Their plan was so focused on getting close to the Creedo duck blind in order to attack them from both sides and they were moving at such a rapid pace once they defeated the Larms, that they probably wouldn't feel the need to check behind them. Therefore, Cadet Jonas Alexander Philpot," said Zach with confidence and sincerity, "you don't ever need to doubt your worth to this team. Captain Mathews' gut feeling about you was right on. If not for you, we would have been discovered, and, most likely, defeated. I, and this whole team, salute you!"

All eleven of the team stood at attention before JA and proudly saluted him.

He returned their salute with a deep-red blush on his cheeks.

As they prepared to advance on the Wyndite team with the bargaining chip they had in Cealdan, his comm unit began to emit words in Salmeaze. Zach looked at JA and asked, "Can you make out what is being said, JA?"

JA's response was to point to Cealdan, whose expression was one of shock and sadness. He then spoke. "By the look on Cealdan's face, I'm sure you can deduce that the news he is receiving is not good," he said with a slight smile appearing on his lips.

Zach eagerly questioned JA further. "What kind of bad news? By the smile on your face, I'd say it's good news for us."

"I'm ten times an idiot!" shouted Ross Carter. "I had it all right here in my pack!"

Keanyn grabbed Ross and looked directly into his face and said, with a great effort to suppress his anger at Ross' outburst, "Keep your voice down, Sergeant Carter. What are you trying to say? Have you got something we need right now?"

"You bet I do, sir!" exclaimed Ross, but in a subdued voice. He continued, "A few weeks ago, I was in the infirmary looking for some medicine for my allergy when the thought struck me. If we were to make it to the Swamp Maneuver, we might need some extra supplies. So I managed to 'persuade' the nurse to give me some extra stuff."

"What kind of extra stuff?" queried Keanyn.

Ross sheepishly replied, "Oh, some needles, gauze, disinfectant, and even a little maloraphine." (This had replaced morphine as a more effective pain killer with no addictive side effects.)

Cheng interjected anxiously, "Let me see if you have enough supplies to give Dooley a fighting chance."

After a quick examination, she sighed and allowed herself a slight smile, saying "I think there's just enough to stitch up nearly all his wounds, or at least the major ones. There's plenty of gauze and bandages. The disinfectant and maloraphine is a God send and should be sufficient."

She cautioned, "That doesn't mean he's out of the woods by any means. This will merely give him time and much needed rest. We must get him to a hospital as soon as we can! His right arm was seriously wounded. I can try to keep the infection in it from spreading, but the arm itself is doubtful."

Keanyn put his head down, rubbing his eyes, saying "He saved my life. I foolishly brought him and four others on this ridiculous mission just to get bragging rights and feather my own nest in order to get a good posting after graduation. That's not worth anywhere near someone's life! Yet that's the price Dooley may have to pay for my vanity and ego!"

A stirring came from Dooley's makeshift cot as he opened his eyes, looked up at Keanyn, and said, "None of us here volunteered for a fool's mission, sir. You are our leader. We believe in you and this mission!" He slowly closed his eyes and fell back into unconsciousness.

Keanyn had regained his composure, grateful for Dooley's impassioned support. But he was still concerned about getting him the complete help he needed as soon as possible. He expressed his concern to Cheng.

"Do you think we need to abort the mission in order for Dooley to survive, Cheng? I am fully prepared to do that. We can accept a figurative casualty within the parameters of this operation, but real casualties are unacceptable!"

Cheng sat still, in thought. When she looked up at Keanyn and the three other sets of eyes, she said, "I'm too young to have had a lot of experience in assessing someone's chances to live or die, even with my training as a medic. But I do know of my grandmother's example. She suffered a terrible injury in a fall. Her granddaughter's trial for engaging in smuggling activities was due in one week, and there was nothing that was going to keep her from living to see the outcome!" Tears welled up in Cheng's eyes as she related the conclusion.

"When the decision was made to have me and my two cousins enroll in the Legion's schools, she was there to hear it. She was very weak and frail and never fully recovered, but she survived long enough to see me through my first year here. She knew that I would take advantage of my second chance. That is something I would never have wanted her to miss. She died full of peace and happiness."

She shifted her focus to Dooley, saying "Dooley is much younger and stronger. Though his wounds are life threatening, you heard his conviction and determination just now. Do you think his will is strong enough to keep him alive until we can get him to a hospital?"

"That was the best answer you could have given, Cadet Wong," stated Keanyn in a low, husky voice. We move forward with the mission!" Keanyn then outlined an adjustment to their plan.

"With one less person, we need to be stealthier in our approach to the Wyndites. The first thing is to make sure Dooley is as comfortable as he can be and assign two of you to carry the cot. That will be Louise and Tom. Each of you will have your weapons at the ready, but if this works as planned, you shouldn't need them. Cheng, if you feel that you can be parted from your charge, I would like to put your full skills to use."

She answered with a nod and said, "If Louise and Tom can stop and check on Dooley periodically, he should need no more than a half dose of maloraphine once to keep the pain at bay and help him sleep, then I'm good to go."

"Thanks," stated Keanyn appreciatively. He added, "I want you to proceed quietly to the Wyndite position, which I estimate is within a mile. Find the best cover you can. Arm yourself and wait on Ross and me to get there. You will start to pick off one or two Wyndites to get their attention. Then as they prepare to fire on your position, we'll come out of cover behind them and get enough of them to do them in."

"How do I let you know where I am?" said Cheng.

"I think if you check your devices, you will see that the water damage was only temporary. That being the case, I will radio the judges concerning Dooley's situation and our homing devices will allow us to know your position."

Ross Carter added a comment. "Dooley's injuries will go a long way in convincing the judges to think that we were being stalked by gators and why we had to cross through the swamp. Captain, you always seem to land on your feet."

Keanyn commented, "I would much rather have to convince them without Dooley being injured, but we're far from being home free, Ross. Things are looking up, though."

Keanyn radioed the judges, who, for the most part, were sympathetic to their situation. General Beckton, however, needed extra convincing. He was still not sure of their being "herded" through the swamp by gators. He continued to question Keanyn.

"Captain Mathews, it is so unlike gators to hunt in packs, let alone force a group of humans to move in any given direction, unless they are following a keenly distinctive and desirable scent. Did any one of you have anything like that with you?"

All of a sudden Keanyn jumped to the incident of the gator urine being spilled in his lap.

I know the scent of that gator urine is no longer on me, he thought. *But maybe I can use that little incident to convince the general of our need to cross through the Albemarl because of the gators.*

When Kenyan related his story to him, the general became more acquiescent to his explanation.

"Of course, you know I can check your story, Captain," stated Beckton. "But combining that with the unfortunate injuries to Cadet Dooley, I am inclined to accept your explanation."

He continued. "Regardless, you six will remain as receiving minor wounds and any further minor wounds could render you as having major wounds. If any of your team were then to be killed, you would be disqualified. Is that clear?"

"Yes, sir!" exclaimed Keanyn decisively.

He turned back to his team and said, "You heard what the general said, so let's be extra careful. Now, move forward!"

In some forty-five minutes, Cheng had positioned herself in a heavily covered cedar grove on a slightly raised hammock that offered her excellent firing angles. She was able to pick off two of the Wyndites who were on the path leading to the Creedo duck blind.

She, and the rest of the team, had come upon their position as they approached the path. Cheng had heard them whispering as she stealthily crawled through the underbrush. Her training as a scout had proven Keanyn's choice of her to be a smart one.

"I've killed two of them," she whispered in the comm to Keanyn. "They're confused, not knowing where the shots came from. Now's your chance, sir."

Keanyn and Ross, along with Louise and Tom, who had laid Dooley's cot on a soft grassy hammock, moved out onto the path some twenty yards behind the Wyndites. They pulled their weapons and aimed them at the unsuspecting Wyndites as Keanyn declared, "I believe, Captain Sensa, that we have what was frequently called in the old west 'the drop on you.'"

The Wyndite captain turned to face Keanyn's team with bewilderment and said, "How did you ever get behind me, Captain Mathews? We arrived ahead of you and headed east. According to my calculations, our two teams were headed in opposite directions. That means you should have been in front of us, not behind!"

Keanyn explained his plan to Captain Sensa, adding their good fortune in learning about the Wyndite's plan.

As this all sunk into Sensa's brain, he looked at Keanyn and said, "Captain Mathews, I believe you could do with some aid in finishing your plan."

Startled by his words, Keanyn asked Sensa, "Are you saying you are willing to help us flush out the Creedos? I appreciate the offer, but as a defeated team, you can't help us fight them or take any other active role."

The Wyndite captain smiled and explained his offer, "We have wanted to wipe that condescending smirk off the faces of the Creedos as much as you. You have never won the Swamp Maneuver, but we have won on two previous occasions, and I might add, not always strictly following the rules. So, if you can win it, that will be nearly as satisfying to us. Therefore, if there is some way we can assist you in this endeavor, we will."

Keanyn anxiously looked at Sensa and said, "I have a badly injured man who fought with a gator. His right arm is the worst. Deep cuts and infection have, I believe, left him on the brink of losing that arm, and perhaps his life, unless we can get him to a hospital ASAP. If I could have two of your team to use that phenomenal speed of yours to carry him out of the swamp to the base hospital, I would be extremely grateful."

Captain Sensa gazed at Keanyn with compassion and said, "I'll get my two speediest men on it!"

Once they secured Dooley onto the cot on which he had been laying, the two Wyndite speedsters took him directly out of the swamp beyond the sight and smell of the Creedos.

After Dooley's departure, Keanyn addressed Sensa again. "Thank you so much for your help, Captain. But I believe you had another offer you wanted to make."

"That's right, Captain Mathews. We can help you without breaking the rules. Though they might get bent a bit. This is how I propose to do it."

He outlined a plan in which he would radio ahead to his other team that there was a strong group of gators advancing on them, forcing them toward the Creedo position. This would serve two purposes.

First, it would enhance the impression that gators were really coming at the Creedos, when Keanyn and his team begin spreading the gator urine around, and second, help convince the judges, who were listening in, that Keanyn's claim of a gator attack was genuine.

Sensa began to radio ahead to Larmuth's team, in code, concerning their defeat by the Earth team. This is the message JA and the rest heard over Cealdan's comm unit after they had captured him.

Not using these precise words, as it was coded so that the judges wouldn't know what they were up to, Captain Sensa said, "I'm sorry to say but we have been surprised by a portion of the Earth team and have suffered too many fatal blows and wounds to remain qualified. I have offered to help Captain Mathews to defeat the Creedos by means of a ruse and a passive ambush. The ambush is where you come in. Take your team and fan out across the path. Your purpose is just to block the path and slow down what should be a fairly frantic retreat by the Creedos."

He then explained his bogus report of a gator attack and Keanyn's use of the urine to flush out the Creedos. He concluded the message with, "As the Creedos retreat, they will run into your team and get bogged down trying to get through. Captain Mathews' team can catch up with them and the other half of his team, coming from the other direction, and squeeze the Creedos in a pincer movement and make short work of them."

Larmuth responded in code as well.

"Captain Sensa, I've just been informed by my rear guard, Cealdan, that he has already been captured by the Earth team and is only a few hundred yards behind our position. They should be ready to carry out the pincer movement in a matter of minutes."

As Captain Sensa relayed this information to Keanyn and his team, they nearly shouted out and jumped for joy. After restraint from Keanyn, he said to them, "Don't go counting your chickens before they're hatched. While this gives us a tremendous advantage, for which we can be extremely grateful to Captain Sensa and his troops, it's not a done deal! We must begin spreading the gator urine and hope it has the desired effect. Then we have to pursue them so that they can run into the waiting arms of Zach's team."

At the Creedo duck blind, Captain Tarth was approached by one of his team who understood Salmeaze and had hacked into the Wyndite frequency. He stated very nervously, "Captain, it seems that the Wyndites have reported being attacked by a group of gators, and since we know they are only about one-half mile away, those gators could make it here!"

Captain Tarth's reply was, "Don't overreact, Cadet Bando. That's just a ruse to scare us. You know gators hardly ever venture out of the center of the swamp, and then it's usually just one. Besides, we would be able—" he paused and continued more slowly "—to smell them if they were . . . Oh my! Can't you smell that? It's gator, and it's getting stronger!"

He and Bando began to panic and run, resulting in all the Creedos rushing to get out of the duck blind. They tried to retreat in an orderly fashion, but it was more like barely controlled chaos.

As Keanyn, Ross, and Cheng spread the gator urine judiciously on plants, rocks, or any surface where it would soak in and smell to high heaven, they began to hear stirrings from the Creedo's position not one hundred yards ahead. There was a moderate breeze that was in their favor, carrying the scent directly toward the duck blind. In less than a minute, they were rewarded by the sight of nearly a dozen Creedos desperately trying to escape from the blind.

They had been joined by the six or so others who had been waiting to ambush any unsuspecting teams who happened to venture into their trap. Except that this time, they were the unsuspecting team who had been maneuvered into retreat.

Ross excitedly said to Keanyn, "It looks like your plan is working, Captain. I mean, look at those Creedos run. I thought I'd never see the day!"

"Just keep spreading that pee and stay out of sight," reminded Keanyn. "We've got to get them headed toward Zach's team and then we'll have them!"

Zach Demopolis checked that his troops were well-hidden in the brush to either side of the path behind the lounging Wyndites who were nonchalantly blocking the Creedo's retreat.

They were heard before they could be seen. The sound of running and tripping feet along with panicked cries announced the arrival of the Creedos.

In just a few more seconds, the jumble of fear-filled Creedos came into view, led by their "fearless" leader Tarth. Unintelligible sounds emanated from their mouths. When they saw the Wyndites sprawled across the path, they screeched (figuratively) to a halt.

Captain Tarth frantically waved his arms and shouted, "What are you doing here, and why aren't you shooting at us?"

Larmuth stepped forward and said, "Because the other part of our team, which was on the other side of your duck blind, was defeated by a small group of the Earth team, who happen to be coming up behind you now."

When the Creedos turned to face Keanyn's small group of five, Tarth grinned and had his team pull out their weapons ready to eliminate the outnumbered Earth troops.

Before he opened fire, he stopped and said, "Wait a minute! Where are the gators? I can still smell them!"

Keanyn stopped and said, "Oh, you mean this gator urine we've been spreading? We've just been playing a little joke on you. But the rest of my team, who now stands behind you ready to fire, AIN'T NO JOKE!"

At that, twelve pseudo-laser guns blasted into the stunned Creedos, and the Swamp Maneuver belonged to Keanyn Mathews' Earth team.

Three Weeks Later

Keanyn's team had assembled at a local steakhouse along with his uncle Mark, who had contributed not only the promised one thousand dollars but had added a 250-dollar bonus to anyone who could eat an entire forty-ounce New York strip.

The top contenders were Ross Carter, Tom Palmer, and, of all people, Jonas Alexander Philpot, who was shoveling it in like a bulldozer.

When the competition ended, Tom had won by eating all forty ounces. He had been hard-pressed by JA, who had consumed thirty-eight ounces; Ross had started to slow down at the two-pound point but did manage a respectful thirty-four ounces.

Tom, therefore, maintained his reputation as a champion eater, but it didn't come without cost. Suffice it to say that in the next forty-eight hours, his visits to the bathroom were unforgettable.

As they were enjoying coffee and other after-dinner drinks, both alcoholic and non-alcoholic per the legal age, the conversation turned to the Swamp Maneuver.

Peter voiced the question all of them wanted to ask: "Keanyn, you and Zach were the only ones from the team to meet with the Judges Panel when they were deciding whether to award us the trophy for not only the Swamp Maneuver but as champions of the entire competition. How did you convince them that we deserved to win?"

Keanyn had the attention of everyone in the private dining room as he answered. "The first thing I noticed was we didn't have to convince every one of the judges. There were three in particular that needed more assurance of our victory. General Beckton, Admiral Kuln from Raushdon, and an individual I wasn't familiar with named Ambassador Yahnsoof Callurran, a top-notch negotiator from Saffo V. They all had undisguised doubt written all over their faces."

Zach interjected a comment at this point. "It was as if they were the only three that mattered as far as receiving a positive judgement was concerned. Frankly, I felt we would be fighting a losing battle trying to convince them."

"So did I!" Keanyn agreed. He went on. "It didn't prove to be as difficult as it had appeared at first. General Beckton and Ambassador Callurran put up fairly strong objections, especially about the validity of our gator attack. And since that was indeed a fabrication to start with, the actual attack on Dooley—coupled with his injuries—helped make the story more acceptable. By the way, Dooley, how are things coming with the physical therapy?"

"The therapy's rough, but it's working," stated Dooley. "They keep talking to me about a prosthesis, but I'm not sure I want one."

The damage to Dooley's right arm had been too severe,

especially with the infection it had received from the extended time he had remained in the swamp before they could enlist the aid of the Wyndites.

When Keanyn learned that Dooley's arm had been amputated, he came straight to the gator stalker's room in the hospital. As soon as he walked into the room, Dooley raised his left arm, palm out to stop Keanyn in his tracks and said, "Now, before you go a-whinin' on about how sorry you are, you know I never wanted for you to give up on the Swamp Maneuver because of me. Schucks! I'da been glad to lose both my arms to have gained the victory we accomplished. Besides, as soon as they got me to the hospital, the doc examined me and said it was too late for the medivac. The infection in my arm was too extensive. That's okay, Keanyn. I told you to keep with the maneuver and not to worry about me. Cheng did a fantastic job with the supplies she had. I do have one regret, though. I just wish I'da got to see the look in Tarth's purple eyes when Zach and his team mowed 'em down. That would have been worth more than the loss of my arm. So don't go fawning all over me!"

Now, as Keanyn looked with deep gratitude across the table at newly-promoted Captain Dooley Paxton, he smiled and said, "Now, just why don't you want a prosthesis, Captain Paxton?"

Dooley responded, "It's not that I don't think it would do any good. It's just that my daddy lost his left arm and never got no prosthesis. With me losing my right arm, it makes us look complete when we stand side by side." He added, "Besides, he says I have a badge of honor like him now, and I kinda like that!"

The room exploded in laughter and applause as Dooley sat down with a deep blush and sheepish smile on his face.

Keanyn's uncle, Mark Mathews, spoke up to get the

attention of the others and said, "We have yet to receive a full explanation of what happened when you and Zach met with the Judicial Panel, Keanyn."

Keanyn began, "Once Beckton and Callurran began to accept our story about being chased by gators into the swamp, the discussion began to turn to the unnecessary restrictions some of the rules put on the teams. We argued that the restrictions about crossing through the swamp did not represent a realistic portrayal of combat conditions nor truly test the leadership and decision-making abilities of the cadets when having to take action when making difficult and dangerous decisions."

"What was their reaction to that?" queried Marjorie.

"Surprisingly positive. Especially from General Beckton," answered Zach. "That seemed to turn the tide in our favor. In fact, it was as if the General had been waiting for that kind of response from us. Is that how you felt, Keanyn?"

"Absolutely!" said Keanyn. "In fact, I was wondering if you had picked up on that as I did."

As Zach nodded in agreement, Keanyn turned a pensive gaze toward the ceiling, and when he looked back on the gathered throng, there was a warm smile on his face as he said, "While the tide had begun to turn, we still weren't out of the woods until Captain Sensa spoke on our behalf. He had insisted on being at the meeting, saying he had important information that could determine the outcome of the matter."

Louise excitedly asked, "What did you think he was going to say?"

Keanyn chuckled as he said, "I wasn't sure, but as he and his team had been such a positive factor in helping us achieve our victory, I felt it had to be something good."

He continued, "Captain Sensa eloquently reported on

the ambush of his team and our subsequent resourcefulness and bravery in flushing out the Creedos and driving them into the waiting arms of Zach's team. The Wyndite captain fervently testified that if there was still any doubt that we had been forced to cut through the middle of the swamp by attacking gators, even with the evidence of Dooley's injuries, the fact that he had himself reported that the gators were continuing their attack should convince anyone that our reports were genuine!"

As they later filed out of the restaurant, Zach approached Keanyn and asked him, "What did General Beckton say to you when we were leaving the Judges Panel chambers after they awarded us the winning trophy?"

Keanyn's reply was that the general had asked him to come to his office at 18:30 hours that evening to discuss something very important. When Zach asked him what they discussed, Keanyn said, "I think that's best left for another time, Zach."

Chapter 6

Robert

The Galactic Legion's Military Police and Security School graduation of 2217 was being held in the modestly sized but richly appointed Morrisy Hall. The hall's auditorium had 2,055 plush, velvety cushioned seats. Crystal chandeliers hung from a ceiling with star-like lights, whose radiance was reflected by the crystals.

The stage, though, was the focal point of the auditorium. The sixty-foot-wide and hundred-foot-deep stage, sitting eight feet above the orchestra pit and six feet above the first four rows of seats, commanded attention.

What really drew the eye to the stage were its four rows of curtains leading to the fifth and final curtain, which covered the entire width and three-fourths the height of the rear wall.

Each of the four rows were opened on either side, with

each row being a little less open than the preceding one, making for a stair-step appearance. Their colors were a dark blue with gold trim on the first row, progressing to a royal blue with silver trim on the last row.

The fifth curtain was that of a beautiful ocean sunset, with the solar sphere seemingly sitting halfway in the blue waters.

What made this scene especially effective was that the sun was positioned directly behind the speaker's lectern. Anyone's eyes would be drawn toward that sun and right on the speaker's face.

Seated on that stage was Robert Porter, who was graduating first in this current class and had just finished his valedictory speech. He was a moderately good-looking eighteen-year-old, standing six feet tall with medium brown hair, a small cleft in his chin, and a slightly muscular physique.

The most striking aspect of his appearance, though, was his bright green eyes. It could be very disconcerting if you came under the scrutiny of those eyes. You might feel anything from guilt or embarrassment to thinking he found you the most fascinating person on Earth. He would always follow that look with a warm smile.

His address had mentioned, "While we cannot possibly predict all the twists and turns our enemy's machinations will take, we must use all the knowledge we currently possess to project, with reasonable accuracy, to the culmination of those machinations.

"That is why I am predicting that the Legion will consider updating and revamping the current intelligence gathering methods in communication, covert operations, and cyber security, especially as they apply to current in-mission starships!"

He finished his oratory on a positive note by saying "This epoch-making innovation will come! I have every confidence in the Legion researchers that they will achieve the cutting-edge technology by means of artificial and natural intelligence. This will, in essence, recreate the intelligence gathering community! And that, fellow graduates and faculty, promises a bright future for space exploration!"

Despite the standing ovation he received, some there questioned his conclusions.

Some three days later, he was approached by two representatives from the Legion's Terran Intelligence Council, or TIC. They encountered Robert as he was leaving the dean's office on a sunny Monday afternoon.

"Are you Robert Porter?" said one of the agents. "My name is Kenneth Crawley, special agent for TIC," as he flashed his credentials for Robert's inspection. He was a five-foot-eight, dark-haired, thirty-something-year-old man of stocky build, with a permanent two-day growth of beard and disapproving scowl.

Good grief, thought Robert. *I couldn't have come up with a better stereotype of a government agent than this guy if I tried.*

Agent Crawley continued, "And this is my partner, Agent Grancowski," introducing a tall, thin man of about forty-five, whose soft, kinder face made Robert think of the old ploy "good cop, bad cop."

"To what do I owe the privilege of a special visit from two of TIC's best?" Robert inquired in a slightly sarcastic tone.

"If there is somewhere we can go to have a more private discussion, we'll tell you how 'special' our visit really is," said Crawley with a mirthless smile on his face. However, it wasn't the insincere smile that unnerved Robert. It was the look he perceived in Crawley's eyes, a look that said, "have your fun now, kid, I'll chew you up and spit you out later!"

Fifteen minutes later, the three men were sitting in a secluded booth at a small coffee bar frequented by students, and since it was 2:30 in the afternoon, most students were in classes. In fact, there was only one other table occupied at that hour and it was in the front portion of the establishment. Therefore, the conditions were excellent for a private conversation.

"It seems that the comments from your valedictory address came to the notice of the director of TIC," Agent Crawley said as he began the discussion. "What Director Novak would like to know is why you feel that our 'intelligence gathering methods' need updating and revamping? That seems to imply that you know something about our intelligence gathering methods, and that makes Director Novak a bit nervous. It's not common for one of the general public to be so well-informed. It tends to undermine the secretive methods that are required to gather that intelligence. Would you care to explain?"

What Robert could say in explanation was much. What he would say was another matter entirely. What he could say had to do with an association his father, Gerald, had as the head of security for Pickle's Investment and Procurement Entity, or PIPE, a hugely successful real-estate investment company that had made its owner, Clarice Pickle, the world's first trillionaire. She was the former Clarice Downing, the daughter of the British Horse Racing Authority's director, Martin Downing.

Clarice was moderately attractive with an oval face that had soft features highlighted by full lips, a strong chin, and a winning smile. Her hair was an almond color with natural body that other women would kill for.

Because of Gerald Porter's close association with the Pickles, his son, Robert, had been the recipient of a first-class education and had made some very interesting connections in the security industry. Through his father's tutoring and his own keen intelligence, Robert had displayed a deep understanding for undercover operations and security from an early age. He had also been mentored by two others affiliated with PIPE.

Clarice had introduced him to ND and her son Stenn. ND—for that was all she would reveal about her identity—aside from being Stenn's mother, was a willowy five feet, ten inches, with long black tresses streaked with golden blonde. Her voice was soft but commanding at the same time. It was difficult to tell when she was being sarcastic or sincere. Stenn, who was sixteen years old at the time and standing six feet tall with medium long, very dark hair and, as Robert came to discover, always clothed in charcoal-gray attire, resembled his mother greatly.

The three of them hit it off immediately. ND and Stenn had been used by Clarice in corporate espionage to both dig up unscrupulous activity by the competition and to protect PIPE from unwanted scrutiny.

Through these two, Clarice wanted to find out if Robert was merely intending to follow his father in security or to branch out into espionage.

In their discussions, Robert had made it clear that he wanted to do more than security and law enforcement. So, ND and her son had decided to take on the task of training Robert in the various aspects of information gathering.

When Robert had asked if there would be any need for him to get formal schooling at the Military Police and Security School, Stenn answered, "We need someone who is official and recognized by the 'powers that be' and can access files and departments that we can't. That's where your formal schooling would pay off. But Mother and I need to stay unofficial in order to get into places and get information you couldn't. That way we get our cake and eat it too."

Robert still had some skepticism as he said, "What if I get caught feeding information to unofficial sources? That could get me drummed out of the business and I definitely wouldn't want to risk that!"

ND replied in an understanding tone, "We wouldn't ask you to do something to jeopardize your career. We haven't told you this yet, but we have the backing of someone very influential, and they have a contact who is very high up in the Intelligence hierarchy. There is little to no risk that if they catch you feeding information to us that you will be punished."

"Little to no risk?" queried Robert.

"Virtually none," said Stenn.

"I can see you two are going to be a lot of fun to work with," said Robert with a chuckle in his voice.

Obviously, Robert couldn't tell the TIC agents all of that. What he did tell them was this, "I know that TIC is aware of my background with my father and his preparation of me for the security and intelligence field. Then there's the obvious evidence of my just having graduated from the Legion's Military Police and Security School. So, a valedictory address about security and intelligence gathering is kind of expected. Why the inquisition?"

Agent Grancowski answered in a soft but firm voice, "Most valedictory addresses from the MP&S School don't hint at having knowledge of the inner workings of the Intelligence community. If you hope to be employed by that community, we hope you are able to keep your exuberant comments to yourself."

His smile was not only mirthless like Crawley's but even more sinister.

Well, so much for "good cop, bad cop", thought Robert. *I guess I'm going to have to call on ND's contact already.*

Chapter 7

The Postings

The early years of the twenty-first century saw a pandemic the likes of which hadn't occurred since 1918–1920. The latter half of the century witnessed some of the worst hurricanes ever that devastated the eastern coast of Florida. Three category fours and two category fives from Ft. Lauderdale to Daytona turned beach erosion into street and neighborhood destruction.

Further storms made it impossible for these areas to bounce back. Especially affected were the Coco Beach and Cape Canaveral areas, forcing the old government agency of NASA to relocate its launch facilities.

They wanted to stay on the East Coast and chose a site less than 250 miles north at Tybee Island, Georgia, because this area had a history of fewer and less devastating hurricanes.

Tybee had also become a ghost town due to rumors of an old WWII, vintage atomic bomb sitting in the waters near the island and a salvage operation that could, possibly, detonate it, if handled improperly.

Since those rumors were started and perpetuated by the US Navy, Coast Guard, and the Georgia Ports Authority, who evacuated Tybee and nearby Wilmington Island, the inhabitants believed the rumors, and few ever came back. This resulted in the navy and coast guard, with the backing of the federal government, commandeering the two islands and buying out the majority of homeowners, only allowing a small number of previous residents to return.

All of this was so that NASA could build its new launch facilities on Tybee with administrative offices and astronaut-training facilities on Wilmington Island.

That was in 2092, and by 2118, the United States, along with all of its agencies—including NASA—were replaced by one of the world's three consolidated "super nations."

The former US, Canada, Mexico, and the Caribbean islands of Cuba, Puerto Rico, the Dominican Republic/Haiti, the Bahamas, and several more had formed the United Affiliation.

The two other "super nations" were made up of a European/North African consolidation and an Asian/Southeast Asian alliance.

The global emphasis had been given to space exploration with the three super nations vying for supremacy.

The United Affiliation had formed UFIE, or the United Foundation of Interplanetary Exploration, which took over all of NASA's former properties.

With the arrival of the Galactic Legion in 2189, UFIE's facilities had been upgraded and included for use as Legion facilities.

Therefore, it was at the Shepard Banquet Hall in the Yeager Wing of the Mendoza complex of the Legion's East Coast Interplanetary Training Facility on Wilmington Island, Georgia, that a very important event was about to take place: The postings banquet for the upcoming launch of the Starship *Cosmic Mall,* and its maiden voyage.

Shepard Hall was a large and beautifully appointed banquet facility. It had a rear wall of ceiling-to-floor windows made of materials brought in from the Prentorian planet of Vendax, which made the "glass" unbreakable, even if hit by a Tragoshun torpedo, which was known to destroy the strongest lead wall.

The side walls of the hall consisted of murals depicting scenes of Earth's past space explorations. The other wall depicted the super nations' various exploits during the twenty-second century, culminating in the final battle around the moons of Jupiter.

That battle raged for two years with no winner and convinced the rulers of the super nations that much more could be accomplished by uniting in a single global government in 2162.

That is what caused the Galactic Legion to take notice of the Earth.

Beside the colorful, eye-catching murals, Shepard Hall's speaker platform was raised three and a half feet above the floor. It ran the full ninety-foot width of the hall with mock-ups of the Mercury, Gemini, and Apollo capsules and the moon lander with a large blank wall at the rear. It was not really a blank wall but was a gigantic telescreen for the visual entertainment of the attendees.

The Shepard Banquet Hall was about to host a very important commission, indeed a historical one worthy of its own mural among the other history-making events depicted.

When a starship had been commissioned for duty, the posting of its officers, both commissioned and noncommissioned, was made public in the form of a posting dinner ceremony. Those who were hoping to receive such an honor were invited to attend but not guaranteed the results they anticipated.

In order to be invited to such a dinner, the hopeful candidates would either have logged many years on lesser starships, gaining experience serving in various capacities, or were recent graduates of the various training schools and programs offered by the Galactic Legion. Such graduates would have finished a fifteen-to-eighteen-month active assignment aboard any number of interstellar training ships. Both their in-school and post-graduate behavior had been assessed, and decisions concerning their postings had been determined.

The Galactic Legion's Starship Fleet had just commissioned the new starship, "MSIII-CM1," the *Cosmic Mall*. It was scheduled for launch on August 24, 2219. The postings dinner was being held on the evening of June 8, 2219, and promised to be one of the most eventful evenings on the recent Legion social calendar.

Many dignitaries from both the earth and other Legion member planets were scheduled to attend. Foremost among the earth dignitaries was the newest and only Earth member of the Legion's Executive Planning Council, General Anthony Beckton. Dr. Carlotta Simmons, the earth scientist who had been the driving force behind the decision to accept the Legion's offer to join. And Mrs. Clarice Pickle who had, just a week earlier, been made the owner/operator of the mall itself.

Off-planet dignitaries included Grand Admiral Haffen Hoo Wangrung, which wasn't really his name but was the closest thing in English to his actual name when it was pronounced in his native tongue of Galrelsh. Admiral Wangrung was from the planet Delfine in the Alfa Centauri system. He was the senior member of the Executive Planning Council and had been the one whose vote to invite the earth into the Legion had been the deciding one.

Two more alien officials headed up the senior pundits that would occupy the speaker's dais: Professor Yargh, the learned expert on fusion-powered propulsion and co-creator of the new Trilliatide power engines that would make their debut in the new starship. Also, Ambassador Yahnsoof Callurran, a highly respected diplomat who had been a mild detractor of the Earth project in the beginning but was now a staunch supporter.

Following the cocktail hour and dinner came the posting ceremony itself.

Brief addresses by Dr. Simmons and Ambassador Callurran were followed by a rather lengthy discourse by Mrs. Pickle, who was tactfully interrupted by the MC, Admiral Wangrung.

"I'm certain we are all looking forward to the shopping and entertainment extravaganza that you will provide via the new Starship *Cosmic Mall*."

He spoke this in clearly understandable English, which very few there thought he was capable of doing. They thought he could speak only the most rudimentary form of the language. They were now embarrassed knowing he had understood them every time they had mimicked him.

He began to speak in a formal tone. "Ladies and gentlemen of both the earth and the many worlds of the Galactic Legion represented here this evening. As Master of Ceremonies for this postings dinner, it would normally be my privilege to make the postings announcements. I am going to relinquish that privilege to one on this dais who has worked tirelessly for the advancement of Earth's endeavors in cooperation with the Legion and its directives. He has also watched and guided many of you recent graduates in your quest to gain a posting on the new starship or one of its support vessels. In addition, he has been a commander and companion to many of you seasoned veterans.

"His most recent distinction as the first Earth member of the Executive Planning Council stands as a testimony to his dedication and passion for the success of this Earth mission. I give you, General Anthony Beckton!"

Thunderous applause and a standing ovation followed this ringing introduction as the general walked to the podium.

As the ovation died down, he began to speak.

"My esteemed colleagues, friends, and candidates, along with all of your friends and supporters. I warmly thank Admiral Wangrung—sorry about the mispronunciation." There was a fair amount of laughter at this aside, and it is to be noted that the admiral himself was among the hardiest participants.

"I doubt that I can fully live up to your glowing endorsement. Nevertheless, I am honored and humbled and will do my best to demonstrate my dedication for what we have and will achieve. I warmly thank those who have already contributed as well as those who will contribute to the success of the Starship *Cosmic Mall*." More loud applause followed this statement. The general paused, then continued to speak.

"The following individuals who will be receiving postings on either the main starship or any of its support vessels should consider themselves pioneers in the earth's association with the Galactic Legion. Not only will you be forging a new historical path in interstellar exploration, but you will be setting a standard for future projects of this kind."

The audience became much quieter as they sensed the general moving toward the crux of his discourse.

After a brief pause, Beckton continued. "I know many of you personally and many others by reputation and I can say that these postings are being filled by the finest we have, and I do not doubt that you will do yourselves and your planet proud as you fulfill your duties."

For the next thirty minutes, the general announced several postings to the four support ships that would accompany the mall ship.

These ships consisted of a lead ship that would function as an introductory, or preview, vessel. Its duties would mostly consist of public relations to smooth the way and prepare the planet's inhabitants for the unique experience they would have with the visit of the mall ship. This ship was called the *Crocket,* after the famous scout Davy Crocket.

Two notable postings on the *Crocket* were Zach Demopolis as it's captain and Marjorie Littleton as second-in-command. During The Swamp Maneuver, these two had discovered how well they worked together and that continued during their fifteen months of training afterward.

Another posting of interest was that of Captain Dooley Paxton as commander of the fourth support ship called—of course—the *Gator*.

It would serve as a very important rear guard and function as protection for the small convoy of starships. In this capacity, it would be the only heavily armed ship in the convoy. If nothing else, Dooley knew how to keep a vigilant rear guard.

When his appointment was announced, Dooley patted his new high-tech prosthetic right arm and leaned toward

Keanyn and Zach, saying "Let's see what kind of paces we can put this highfalutin' piece of machinery through on this job!"

The other two smiled at Dooley's brand of "down home" humor.

The two other ships would serve as supply ships for the mall and its crew. Thus, the *Mall's* 636 retail outlets and numerous eateries would stay well-stocked.

Each of the two ships would rotate in regular intervals, making supply runs to space ports and Legion facilities. They would, also, carry any mall staffers and starship crew members who had leave to the Legion port they were going to for "R&R".

Now came the time for the postings to the main vessel. General Beckton paused and looked out over his excited and expectant audience. His gaze may have lingered over table seventeen where Keanyn and his team, along with Mac, Stella, Grannison, and Edward were sitting on the edge of their chairs. He breathed a deep sigh, slowly blinked his eyes, and began.

"To be a captain of a major starship, let alone the first in a historic endeavor, could be said to be daunting. But I say to you, ladies and gentlemen, that the individual chosen to captain the Starship *Cosmic Mall,* will not find it daunting but will view it as the unequaled challenge to which he feels equal."

Many gasped at this comment wondering what kind of upstart was going to be appointed. Others, who knew the general better appreciated the respect Beckton had for this, yet to be named, captain.

The general continued. "The time I have spent both observing and interacting with this young man has proven to be exciting, exhilarating, frustrating, and downright maddening. But the results he obtains and the loyalty he engenders from those under his command are something I have not seen in decades!

"Therefore, I give you the commander of Earth's contribution to the Galactic Legion, the Starship *Cosmic Mall*." Beckton paused, extending his hand toward table seventeen, and said, "Captain Keanyn Mathews!"

The hall erupted in shouts, whistles, and applause as—first table seventeen, followed by the entire audience—rose in honor of this prestigious appointment.

Keanyn himself was humbled and overwhelmed for, perhaps, the first time in his life.

Zach, who was sitting next to Keanyn, gave him a high five and said, "It couldn't happen to a nicer guy, and better you than me."

As the excitement died down, Beckton cleared his throat loudly and continued with the postings.

"Second-in-command and chief pilot of the starship will be one whose record of interstellar missions makes him an excellent choice. Indeed, his father proved to be a great influence on my career." By saying this, the general added a personal note to the appointment. He added, "We have concentrated on an element of youth for many of these postings and our reasons for such are well known. But experience and maturity are still elements that are highly valued. In view of that, we have chosen Commander Grannison Loche as second-in-command."

This was met with much clapping, especially from the older attendees. A respectful standing ovation was forthcoming as well.

"It is now my great privilege to call on Professor Yargh to announce the posting of head science officer. I do this not only due to the professor's esteemed position in the science community but also because of his close association with this appointee's work and accomplishments. Professor Yargh, please."

Modest but respectful applause greeted the professor as he took the podium and began speaking.

"I am sure that it has not gone unnoticed that many of the accomplishments and discoveries that have taken place after the Galactic Legion arrived on your planet have contained little recognition for the contributions made by those native to this planet."

This statement was met with much trepidation, some confusion, and just a little anger and suspicion by a small group of dissenters sitting at table 114.

The professor pushed forward. "I assure you; we intend to amend that beginning with this next appointment." He stopped and looked out on his highly intrigued audience and said, "For some time, the Legion engineers and physicists have wrestled with the problem of power interruptions in the light-speed drive of our propulsion systems, especially when traveling through solar systems with cooler burning G and K suns, as is yours.

"The problem appeared if our ships traveled at less than light speed through the system and attempted to power up to light speed afterward. Of course, the problem would be exacerbated if we spent time docked at some point within that system. As your solar system is one of the several with G or K suns, and we have had a lot of our ships docked here following our invitation for you to join the Legion, we decided to address the problem aggressively."

He turned his gaze upon table seventeen as he reached the apex of his speech and said, "One of my more gifted students had already demonstrated her ingenuity in developing the now famous space adhesive, EM 304, which, I am led to believe, stands for two ancient adhesives and something called an area code from the old-fashioned communication system of the twentieth and early twenty-first centuries. In any case, it is remarkably strong and efficient, and the student never received the full credit she deserved."

More uncomfortable chair shifting, and nervous coughing accompanied these statements. Some wondered if Yargh was purposely trying to discredit himself or gearing up for a full-blown breakdown. He was pushing against all the current understanding and policies. Surely the Planning Council could not be approving of the line of thought this speech was taking. The professor acknowledged the uneasiness by pausing, staring down the dissenters, and continuing.

"Well, ladies and gentlemen, I am here to say that not only will she now get the credit she deserves for that discovery, but she will also receive the bulk of the credit for discovering and developing the solution for the light-speed problem in G and K star systems with the invention of Trilliatide," he stated proudly while nearly a third of the audience gaped in utter consternation and disbelief.

Amid this reaction, the professor inclined his head and made a rising motion with his hands toward table seventeen as he said, "Miss McCardle Stinson, please stand up!"

Mac was completely dumbfounded as her father took her arm and helped her to stand as the other two-thirds of the audience clapped, cheered, and pounded their cups on their tables, anticipating the announcement. Finally, recognition was being given to the accomplishments of earthlings.

Professor Yargh stated proudly, "It is my happy task to present to you the head science officer of the Starship *Cosmic Mall,* and the chief developer of 'Trilliatide,' Lieutenant commander McCardle Stinson."

Most of the diners joined in another round of cheering

and applause, the disgruntled attendees from table 114 headed for the door in disgust, when, suddenly, Admiral Wangrung stepped to the microphone and said in a strong, stern voice, "In case any of you on your way out are planning to report tonight's proceedings as a violation of formal Legion policy, I can assure you that the decisions expressed here have the full consent and approval of not only the Planning Council but the majority of the governing entities both on and off planet."

More loud cheers and ovations followed this announcement as Mac, Grannison, and Keanyn, meeting for the first time aside from their formal introductions at the beginning of the banquet, put their arms around each other in a wonderful show of solidarity.

In the midst of this camaraderie, Keanyn leaned his head into the circle of new friends and said, "Nice to meet you. It's gonna be great working with you."

Grannison said, "Maybe I can learn a thing or two from you youngsters."

Other postings of note included the communications officers for the mall ship and the *Crocket*.

Because of his high level of intelligence in the use of diplomacy, Jonas Alexander Philpot was assigned as the comm officer on the mall ship. Peter Dubois' linguistic skills were recognized by his appointment of communications officer on the *Crocket*. Peter had added five more alien languages to his repertoire for a total of twenty-four.

The position on the *Crocket* was, perhaps, more critical than that of the mall ship since it would be going in advance of the main vessel, acting as a liaison and diplomatic buffer for the mall. The success of the communications the

Crocket would have with the mall ship's next port-of-call would be crucial to the welcome it would receive, not to mention the success of its retail sales.

Another posting that was of interest was that of Edward Butler as secondary navigator for the mall ship. Seeing as he was the half-brother of the ship's second-in-command, he did not receive the position of primary navigator, who would frequently be on the bridge during the same time as his brother, and the Legion's policy of protecting against charges of nepotism as well as lessening the risk of injury from attack to multiple family members was thus observed.

The very large shuttle launching and docking bay needed the skills of a sharp-eyed and sharp-witted individual to manage the frequent comings and goings of the mall when it was docked at a planet and shuttling customers back and forth. The highly competent Lieutenant Cheng Wong had been selected for this task, and she also served as a helper in sick bay when the ship was not docked "for customers."

Mac's roommate, Stella Steel, and their Sharleean friend, Larindoo kwark, had been given positions overseeing the numerous botanical gardens throughout the mall.

Lastly, there was the second-in-command on the *Gator* as well as some of the crew. Wyndite commander, Darmeul Sensa, was appointed as Captain Paxton's second, and among his crew members were Tom Palmer and Louise Munoz, while Lieutenant Commander Ross Carter worked under Commander Robert Porter, head of security for the Starship *Cosmic Mall*.

Chapter 8

Pre-launch

There were twenty-two of them in the officers' mess of the mall ship at nine a.m. on a Monday morning, eleven weeks after the postings dinner. The last eight weeks and four days had been spent feverishly preparing to familiarize themselves with their duties and the systems they would be responsible for on board this gigantic retail wanderer as it sat in the on-deck launch port at the Lunar Launching Site.

For the next ten days, they were required to get to know each other in a more personal environment. After all, if they were to spend the next year working and living closely together but were virtually strangers; how could they trust one another in crucial situations?

Some of them already knew one or two of the others well, but the Legion's Interactive Relations Committee, or

IRC, felt strongly that a command crew's effectiveness was greatly enhanced when they had a strong rapport and a trusting spirit.

Among those gathered that morning were Captain Mathews, Grannison and his brother, Edward, Mac Stinson, Robert Porter, and his assistant, Ross Carter.

Ambassador Yahnsoof Callurran was also in attendance. He had been appointed as the mall ship's chief liaison officer. His well-known diplomatic skills would be put to excellent use in welcoming the various alien officials and shoppers aboard the ship to experience its one-of-a-kind retail cornucopia.

Other bridge crew members at the morning gathering were head navigator, twenty-year-old Carl Burdgess, the twenty-one-year-old, blond-haired amazon, Lindsey Thompson—whose whiz kid computer skills had landed her the post of chief computer systems tech—was present, much to the delight of the male officers.

Further, there was the sturdy, thirty-nine-year-old chief engineering officer, Lieutenant Commander Stokely "Stokes" Davis.

The mall ship's head physician was a thirty-one-year-old Russian named Alfred Karushkin. At the age of twenty-three, he had been on a team of Russian doctors and scientists who had, finally, developed a cure for cancer.

A youthful and mischievous Wheerie from Raushdon named Saffaw was hired as mall manager. Wheeries are humanoid in form, short in stature, with ultra-quick reflexes and furry, muscular legs and long arms (with six fingers and toes).

Clarice Pickle had hired Saffaw because he had a sharp business mind and a knack for getting the most out of transactions.

"If you are going to negotiate a business deal with a Wheerie, and especially Saffaw," noted Clarice, "you had better enter the discussions with plenty of money to lose."

Finally, fellow captains Zach Demopolis and Dooley Paxton, from the *Crocket* and *Gator* respectively, were on hand.

Zach had some burning questions to ask Keanyn, and this might be the last time he could pose them before they launched.

"Keanyn, a little over two years ago, I asked you about General Beckton's appointment to the Executive Council and all you said was that it had answered some questions you had. Would you care to explain what you meant by that?"

Keanyn's reply was preceded by a warm smile. He began.

"In the week or so before the Swamp Maneuver, I had observed the general exhibiting some strange behavior toward his driver and secretary. On two occasions, I happened to be within earshot of him and his driver as they were about to leave his office on his regular ride to HQ and his departure for home at the end of the day. They didn't know that I was there because I was, by chance, around the corner of the building."

Zach interrupted and in an unbelieving tone said, "'By chance'? One time might be by chance, but twice! Knowing you, I don't think so."

Several of the others added their agreement by way of barely controlled mirth and even Keanyn chuckled as he replied.

"Ah! You know me too well, Zach. In fact, I had made it a habit to linger around the General's office at that time of day whenever I could. What I heard him say to his driver was that he wasn't going to base HQ or home. He said he needed to be taken to the base airport as he had to talk to some people at Government HQ. That got me wondering if there were some changes coming down. I really wasn't thinking personnel change, but possibly procedural.

"Then a few days later, I was in the general's outer office when he came out in a hurry to leave and told his secretary to prepare his desk and then broke off when he saw me there. His secretary, Sergeant MacGruder, gave him a knowing look and a slight nod of her head, and that got the wheels in my head turning again. Then when he announced his new appointment that night of the Swamp Maneuver, the coin dropped."

Zach shook his head as he said to Keanyn, "I've said it to you before, my friend, one day that insatiable curiosity of yours will get you in trouble."

"Oh, I think it already has, Zach. I'm sure this little excursion of ours will find plenty of trouble for us. But it promises something better instead. A whole lot of fun and adventure," was Keanyn's reply.

This was just the kind of banter the IRC was hoping for. It was exchanges like this that would give the other officers insight into the personality of their captain and others. This, in turn, would lead to a better understanding of how to deal with one another.

Zach now continued the discussion. "Keanyn, I have one more question, and I think I've shown great patience in waiting this long to ask it."

"I think I know what you're going to ask, Zach, and the time has certainly come to give you the answer," said Keanyn as he shifted to straighten his posture. "You want to know what General Beckton said to me in his office a few hours after the grilling we received from the Rules Committee on our conduct during the Swamp Maneuver."

Zach exclaimed, "Precisely! I mean, the general had asked

you to come to his office right after they decided that we qualified to win the cadet maneuvers for the first time ever, and when I asked you about it later, you had a Cheshire Cat smile on your face and an ornery glint in your eye, but you wouldn't answer my question. You owe me, partner!"

"Indeed, I do," was Keanyn's reply. He continued, "The first thing the general told me came as a complete surprise. He said that he had known my father for a brief time and had observed his leadership qualities and had respected him so much that he had decided to adopt much of my father's methods himself in striving to reach out for a command position."

Grannison now joined in the conversation by saying "That means he knew both our fathers and respected them enough to adopt their methods!" He then became very thoughtful as he rubbed his chin and said, "I wonder if our both being posted to the same starship and even on the bridge together is more than a coincidence?"

Robert chimed in by saying "Are you suggesting that the fix may have been in when it came to the assignment of you two?"

"Nothing that sinister," answered Grannison. "I firmly believe that I qualified for my posting, and from what I've observed of our captain these last ten weeks, he certainly qualified for his."

Grannison was not fully aware of the positive impact this had on not only Keanyn but many of the others gathered in the mess hall. His unsolicited vote of confidence for the captain infused confidence in them that their second-in-command would support the captain, engendering a cooperative spirit among the ship's command. The IRC's implementation of the ten-day, get-to-know period was getting it's intended results already on day one.

Keanyn acknowledged Grannison's comment by a grateful tilt of his head in Grannison's direction. He then continued to answer Zach's question further.

"That's not all General Beckton said to me. He also told me that he had seen my father during the last few days of his life, as he was succumbing to the toxins he had inhaled when he helped pull the soldiers trapped in their wrecked armored Terrain Hover Craft after the vent lines had been breached. They had their masks on. Dad just rushed in to help with no thought for himself."

Keanyn paused as emotions overcame him. The others in the room remained respectfully quiet. Not a few of them shed tears. After a minute or two, Keanyn continued.

"The general told me that my father had talked with him about me and asked him if he could keep an eye on me, as I had aspirations of following him in a military career. He told him that I showed promising leadership skills, but not to smooth my path out. He wanted him to monitor my progress and, if he was in a position to, give me challenges and even some obstacles in order to see if I had the stuff to meet the challenges and overcome the obstacles.

"The general told me he had done his best to make sure I didn't have the smoothest road. He also said that he had seen a lot of himself in me, and that when I had brought up the thought of changing some of the rules in the cadet maneuvers to make them more like actual battle situations, that is what he had been wanting to do for some time but could never find the right moment.

"It seems," continued Keanyn, "that he had anticipated our little ruse in crossing through the swamp and never accepted our, ah, *explanation* about being herded by the gators. He said that his giving you permission to proceed was one of the most difficult decisions he'd ever had to make."

"Why was that?" queried Zach. "I mean if he knew it was a ruse and even anticipated it, I would think he could have made that decision in advance."

Keanyn replied, "Oh, he had already made the decision, but now that it had come time to implement it, he knew that he couldn't turn back from a decision that could very well endanger my life as well as those with me. He agonized that he may have gone beyond what my father had asked of him by putting me in such danger."

"That just confirms the respect and admiration I've had for the general," said Zach. "And knowing that he was probably a bit of a risk taker like you makes me like him even more."

There was a little nervous fidgeting on the part of some in the room when Zach alluded to Keanyn's tendency to take risks. Some of them were very "by the book" individuals and were uncomfortable when people took risks, especially ones in positions of command.

Even this somewhat negative reaction was in keeping with the desired results the IRC was looking for. They believed it was realistic and ultimately healthy for there to be some amount of anxiety and criticism toward command. They felt this merely displayed personality differences that could be overcome.

It must be noted that, while that view is correct to a point, if taken too far, it could cause serious problems.

Lindsey took this lull in the conversation to turn to Mac, who was sitting beside her, and ask, "I know some of the command crew is familiar with how you and Professor Yargh came to discover the solution to the propulsion system problems, but I haven't been filled in. How did you work out the problem?"

Mac smiled softly as she recalled that moment when

the light finally dawned in her mind after sensing that she had been so close for weeks.

"Lindsey," she said, "something as simple as a casual conversation by two of my lab-mates turned my mind in the right direction. One of them was asking the other for some advice with a family issue and this is what the other one said: 'I think you've been looking too far a-field for a solution. Why don't you try looking closer to home?'

"Then it dawned on me," Mac continued. "That's what I needed to do. I had been looking exclusively for an answer from alien chemistry. But then I realized the problem in the propulsion system occurred when the Legion's ships were in solar systems like ours. They probably needed answers from our chemistry and our physics. So as soon as I told Professor Yargh that, he couldn't believe we had all been so blind to the obvious.

"A great deal of progress has been made in the field of quantum chemistry during the last two centuries. The valency—or measure of the combining power of elements with other atoms, forming chemical compounds—has been especially revealing. We had never explored this procedure when it came to Terran elements combining with extraterrestrial ones. When we started to implement this idea, the results were almost immediately positive, though at times, volatile!

"After a few months, we were able to find the proper chemical compound and direct its powerful energy pulse in a nondestructive path toward the propulsion system of a starship with much thanks to both Earth and alien engineers, one of whom is sitting here with us in the person of Lieutenant Commander Stokes Davis. Concentrating on our own physics and its interaction with alien science also reminded me of an earlier conversation I had with Professor Yargh.

"When I first joined Professor Yargh and his team to help them try to find the answer to the light-speed problem, I had made the simple observation that the 'sputtering' engines, as he described them, reminded me of a car engine that sputtered due to its spark plugs being fouled by corrosion or wear. When I started looking at Terran physics and chemistry for a solution, I noticed that the longer a Legion ship was docked in a G or K system, the more it accumulated a kind of buildup of a chemical alloy within the multi-light-speed engines.

"The Legion's scientists either didn't notice it or consider it a factor. The latter is my thought. In fact, I didn't think that it was that significant myself, at first.

"That is, until I asked the engineers, like Stokes, to run some burn tests to see if the MLS engines ran cleaner if they reduced the amount of buildup to normal levels."

Stokley Davis chimed in with his observation. "We had to adjust the burn ratio of some of the fusion formula in order to dissipate the proper amount of buildup. That was done by a very careful trial-and-error method. Too much error could have resulted in disaster. Therefore, the testing took two weeks to arrive at a solution. But when it did, it was amazing to see those MLS engines roar to life in the cleanest burn I've ever seen! Voila! We had solved our annoying problem thanks to Yargh's team and, primarily, our excellent science officer, Lieutenant McCardle Stinson."

Many in the officers' mess hall murmured their appreciation with expressions such as "nice," "super," or "well done."

Lindsey asked, "How did you arrive at the name, 'Trilliatide'?"

Mac answered with a smile and a chuckle. "We used the prefix 'tri' from the word 'trivalent,' which has a direct connection in chemistry to valency. We felt we had discovered a new 'tide' in quantum chemistry and affixed that word to the end. But 'tritide' sounded too simplistic for something that had taken so much effort to accomplish. Then there was our arrogance as scientists that wouldn't allow us to come up with a name with less than three syllables."

Many wondered whether Mac was being serious or sarcastic with that last statement and they weren't sure how to react. It was Edward Butler who broke the tension by saying "If you think that scientists have cornered the market on arrogance, you've never been in a room of pilots. They'll 'drive' you to drink!"

Grannison turned to his brother and said, "That's a good one coming from you. You've always claimed you were smarter than me."

Edward countered with, "That's not arrogance. Just a simple statement of fact."

The room erupted with laughter, and as the mirth died down, Lindsey brought the conversation back to its central point.

"So, Mac, how did you *arrogant scientists* come up with the rest of 'Trilliatide'?"

Mac answered, "This problem had been bothering us for the better part of a week when we turned to a friend of mine in the philology and etymology department. If she couldn't come up with something, no one could."

"And did she?" was Lindsey's excited question.

"In a way, yes," said Mac as she recalled the occasion. She had a broad smile on her face as she answered. "After giving us many suggestions, which didn't seem to fit, I looked at her in frustration and said, 'There must be something you can come up with, Illya!' Then suddenly I stopped. That was it! It flowed off the tongue so smoothly, it made the word complete. TRI-ILLYA-TIDE, with a slight spelling change became 'Trilliatide'!"

Many nodded in approval or laughed softly as Mac finished her story. The Wheerie, Saffaw, whose furry appendages were jiggling with humor, stated, "I thought I was going to be stuck on a ship of boring scientists with no sense of humor. I'm going to have to dig down deeper into my bag of tricks to keep up with you guys."

"I hope you manage to find time to do your work as well," stated his employer, Clarice Pickle, who had just entered the mess hall as Mac was finishing her explanation.

She was wearing a designer pant ensemble. She had decided to dazzle everyone with a Dalwinnia Trontwein creation from the fashion houses of Zarkon, the Planet of Silks in the Ursa Minor sector.

Her plump five-foot, eight-inch frame allowed the satiny material of shimmering aqua and pearl sheen to flow like gentle ocean waves. When you have that much money, you can make anything look good on you.

She turned a look of feigned displeasure on Saffaw and said, "I would hate to have to sack you for, as everyone knows, there's nothing more annoying than an out-of-work Wheerie."

Saffaw, who was rarely disturbed by Mrs. Pickle's jibes, shot back with, "I'm glad you're here, Mrs. Pickle. I am happy to inform you that I filled those last three vacant spaces on the second tier with very good retailers. First, there is the Jal bead chain of Moolyn's from Garsden. They have the best-selling line of Jal beads in their quadrant of the galaxy. I've never seen such vivid iridescence in my life. Then I—or, I should say—my associates landed the Krolmation confectioners, the Panto Brothers. Their Choco/Ryman-flavored bon-bons cannot be duplicated anywhere in the Legion.

"I saved the best for last," he winked conspiratorially and assumed a pose that said, *I'm very proud of myself and you should be too.*

With his thin-lipped mouth set in a confident grin, he said, "I'm sure you know how hugely successful the sporting-goods firm Davidson's has become. I am proud to say that, as its sixth and final anchor store on the second tier, the *Cosmic Mall* welcomes Davidson's first Multi-World Sporting Goods Emporium!"

He could nearly have patted himself on his back with his long arms . . . and almost did.

There were many "oohs," "aahs," and applause that accompanied this announcement. When things quieted down, Mrs. Pickle said, "I hope you didn't spend all the money I gave you for your endeavors on bribing the aforementioned businesses to agree to come on board."

His reply to her last comment was, "Haven't you heard, Mrs. Pickle, that the way to land a potential client isn't about how much you pay but about how much you know?" as he put his index finger on the side of his thin nose.

Having said this, the two of them retired to a far corner table to discuss further business. The rest were left to wonder which one of them would come out on top in a battle of business wits.

While there were many more conversations during that morning, one more is of particular note.

Stokes Davis was asked by Ross Carter what he thought about the design and engineering of the mall starship, and the chief engineer answered with both criticism and praise.

"I had mixed emotions as we coasted into space port and I got my first real look at her. I've served on half a dozen starships in my nineteen years as a military engineer and I can tell you I've never seen one designed as oddly as this one. It's not that it's ugly, just odd. Like I said. The fact that the bridge is so far removed from the fuselage, and it sits on top of a vertical shaft that houses the quarters of the bridge officers, is strange enough. But that vertical shaft is connected to a horizontal corridor that runs in front of the fuselage and you're putting the bridge so far out there that it's like a bullseye that enemy ships will just use for target practice! I mean, the bridge should be elevated somewhat above the body of the ship but not like this one is!"

He continued in this incredulous tone. "I know it's got the most advanced shielding system ever created, but someone will find a way to breach it eventually."

Keanyn interjected, "I noticed that apparent design flaw myself, Stokes, but after working on that bridge for ten weeks, I find the amazingly unobstructed view breathtaking. I almost don't want to use the view screens sometimes."

"You may change that opinion when you encounter hostile fire for the first time," stated the chief engineer. "That being said—there is much that I like about this ship. The placement of the bridge crew's quarters in such close proximity to the command center will ensure quick access to the bridge during an emergency. That will allow for gaining rapid control of any situation."

Stokes Davis smiled widely as he thought back to his close examination of the ship both inside and out. There was a definite sense of awe in his voice when he said, "The fuselage of this ship is so beautifully put together, both inside and out, that I can't help but admire it like a flawless piece of art. The cylindrical structure of its hull is so proportionately aesthetic and ultimately functional that I couldn't stop staring when I first laid eyes on it during our approach to space dock! Then seeing the inner workings of its systems was even more astounding."

He turned to the chief computer system officer and said, "Lindsey, I believe you told me how impressed you were with the efficiency of the computer systems on this vessel."

She responded, "Impressed may be an understatement. I have never experienced as fast, user-friendly, or comprehensive a system of inner ship controls as this one. From communications to climate control and everything in between, this starship is almost effortless to control and monitor. With thought-process controls for inner-ship communications, meal ordering and preparation, entertainment services, and dozens of other functions, 'computer' seems too archaic a word to use."

The thought-process controls operated by using one's mind to access specific services within the ship. Before using these controls, a crew member or mall employee had to be fitted with a cerebral-sensing device. It was placed in a one-inch, pouch-like slot behind the right ear. The sensors within the device synced with one's brainwaves and that person could begin sending and receiving instructions that would enable one to order food, choose what entertainment they wanted, control their personal climate, and other functions.

The senior officers, sick-bay personnel, and mall management were fitted with more complex devices equipped with uses particular to their needs.

Stokes took up the conversation again. "When I saw that those systems had been installed wirelessly, using sensors that ran through the walls of the fuselage with microchip-trip junctions, I asked my electrical engineers how it was possible. They said they were still learning the alien technology."

"Will they be ready to handle it by launch time?" asked Louise Munoz.

"My concern as well," stated Cheng Wong "There are a lot of systems in sick bay that use the thought process controls. I'd hate to think that the life or death of patients would be dependent on the incomplete knowledge of the techs in charge of those systems."

"Not to worry," soothed Stokes. "That conversation I had with the techs was several weeks ago. They have since told me how well their grasp of the system has improved. They have no doubt they'll be ready by launch." He now turned his attention to a totally unique feature of the mall ship.

"How many of you know the complete function of the spherical plate that sits up against the bottom of the horizontal shaft?"

About twelve of the twenty-three people who now occupied the mess hall raised their hands Some three or four appeared to do so uncertainly. Stokes continued, "That plate, whose circumference is one-third of the fuselage, is made of the brand-new generation four Strell. That alloy has been tested to resist a direct hit from a Delfinian Core Blaster missile."

Everyone in the room but Keanyn, Grannison, Robert, as well as ND and her son Stenn, who had been last minute inclusions in the crew at Robert's strong request, gave an audible gasp.

"I see that some of you who thought you knew about the plate did not know everything," stated Chief Stokley Davis. "But that's not all!" he proclaimed.

"The impregnability of that Strell plating makes that plate a perfect battering ram when it is deployed vertically at the bow of the ship. It seems that some of the design engineers happened upon the battering ram scenario as they were researching seventeenth- and eighteenth-century sea battles. Therefore, though this ship may not be equipped with any 'regular' weapons, we do have an 'ace in the hole.'"

Robert Porter stood to get everyone's attention. When the room quieted down, he spoke. "As head of security for this starship, I will tell you that the information Mr. Davis has just given you had been classified with very few aboard the ship aware of it. In just the last twelve hours, it has been declassified. Mr. Davis has chosen to reveal this information to you in his own inimitable way. I must caution you to be very careful to whom, if anyone, you choose to share this information."

Robert gave a not-so-friendly look at the chief engineer and motioned for him to follow him into the private dining area used by visiting dignitaries. Once inside, Robert turned to Stokes and said, with some heat in his voice, "I don't know how you knew that the information concerning the frontal plate had been declassified, but you should have cleared it with me before you made it public! I stopped you from possibly going further and revealing the other uses that plate has."

Stokes was a bit ruffled as he spoke in answer to Robert's reproof. "I was never told that any of the information about this ship was to be kept from the crew itself. And besides, they are going to find out by the time we get to our first port-of-call." As they were both of the same rank, they could address each other without protocol.

"As far as the 'other' uses of the frontal plate are concerned, surely you can see how dangerous that knowledge could be in the wrong hands!" stated Robert emphatically.

Stokes commented, barely holding back his anger, "I am fully aware how sensitive that information is, Lieutenant

Commander! But seeing how everyone currently on board this ship will be eyewitness participants to its capabilities very soon, what's the harm in telling them about its use as a battering ram? And that's the tip of the iceberg when it comes to its main function!"

"And that is just why I stopped you when I did!" exclaimed Robert. "I was afraid you would reveal that information prematurely. Since you know all of that delicate information due to the fact that you are the chief engineer, I would expect you to act with more discretion."

"And I would hope that you would trust me to know better!" stated Stokes. "And if we're being honest, I resent a barely-twenty-year-old kid thinking he knows better than I do! Good night! We have to trust someone who's just reached the age of adulthood with the security of not only this ship, but our very safety? What was the Legion thinking?"

Robert was stung by Stokes' lack of respect for him, but it wasn't totally unexpected. He decided to end the conversation quickly with the thought of resolving their differences at another time. He said,

"As to my credentials, Chief Davis, we can discuss those later in a calmer setting. For now, let's agree to disagree on some of these issues until then."

This statement seemed to settle Stokes down and he replied, "That suits me fine." He had a sheepish look on his face as he added, "I do apologize for my comment concerning your age. If we're going to work together, we need to have respect for each other."

They both smiled and shook hands, but Stokes couldn't help adding a final barb. "I'll look forward to our upcoming chat and getting the chance to set you straight."

"That works two ways, Mr. Davis," noted Robert as the two officers left the room.

Even though this had been a confrontational discussion, now was the time to bring out any differences the officers and crew might have. Better to clear the air before they launched than when they were in the middle of an issue during the heat of the mission.

In the days to come, many more discussions, both amicable and confrontational, would occur between the officers, medical staff, and mall management.

These would prove to be invaluable during the future adventures of the Starship *Cosmic Mall*.

Indeed, the future of this ship and its crew could not have been anticipated by the most experienced of space travelers.

Chapter 9

The Launch

The excitement on the bridge of the mall starship was palpable. Captain Keanyn Mathews was preparing to address all on board. As he sat straight up in the commander's seat, he said to JA Philpot.

"Mr. Philpot, open up all ship level communications, please."

"Aye, sir. All level comms are now open," came the reply from the ship's communications officer.

Keanyn began by addressing the entire ship's company. "We are finally poised at the threshold of discovery. In just a few seconds, we will begin to move out of the space dock and join the four support vessels waiting for us to take our position at the center of the convoy. I know you have all been anxious for this moment since you knew you would be part of this historic venture. Well, it is now here!"

He paused for just a second as he turned to his second-in-command and chief pilot, Grannison Loche. "Mr. Loche, engage starboard thrusters at 15 percent to clear the dock housing."

"Aye, Captain. Engaging starboard thrusters at 15 percent" was Grannison's crisp response. Then he continued. "Ship is clear of dock housing."

From the moment of its conception until this very point in time, the Starship *Cosmic Mall*, had been attached either figuratively or literally to some form of restriction. Now it was fully functional and under its own power. This new freedom was sensed by all on board, but especially by her crew. Therefore, a controlled but determined applause began from the bridge.

The sound of a growing ovation was then heard throughout the ship from all of the areas. First engineering, then the shuttle deck, and when the mall staff added its thunderous applause and cheers, the sound was deafening. When it began to die down, Keanyn whispered to Mac, "I wonder what they'll do when we hit light speed?"

Mac's answer was "I believe I saw several cases of champagne in the chief engineer's cabin."

Keanyn grinned then gave the command, "Engage aft thrusters at 25 percent and proceed forward at eighteen degrees port to exit docking area."

"Proceeding as ordered, Captain," came the pilot's response. After a thirty-two-second wait came Grannison's next statement. "Clear of docking area and ready for full-launch command, sir."

Keanyn said, "Wait for support vessels to confirm their positions."

A new computerized coordination program had been developed by a team of Glebian technicians under the guidance of Communications Officers Philpot and Duboise that enabled the mothership of a convoy to link with all of the ships and act as control for the entire convoy.

Therefore, when the mall ship attained its position at the center of the convoy, Keanyn addressed the captains of the fore and aft vessels. "Captain Demopolis, do you confirm position and up link?"

Zach replied, "Yes, Captain Mathews, we are in position and in sync."

Keanyn then asked the same question of the *Gator's* captain, and Dooley Paxton responded with a quirky grin on his face, "As sure as my daddy and a gator will be together in the swamp hoedown, we are in position and locked on to your gentle embrace."

All eyes on the bridge turned to Keanyn. He did a little shake of his head and looked firmly forward toward the view screens. "Chief Engineer Davis, are all systems go in engineering?"

"Yes, Captain," came Stokes' reply. "And if you don't mind my saying so, sir, we're all raring to go down here."

"Duly noted, Chief." Then Keanyn turned to Grannison and said, "All eyes forward and, Commander Loche, proceed at one-quarter sub-light on the predetermined coordinates."

As everyone on board the Starship *Cosmic Mall* felt the gentle, but unmistakable, thrust of the engines gliding into the solar system, an elated cheer erupted as they began their historical journey.

In the three and one-half days it would take the ship to clear the solar system before jumping to light speed, the officers and crew would acclimate themselves to carrying out their duties while in actual space flight.

This gave the management and employees of the mall time to get their "sea legs" as well. Many of them were experiencing space travel for the first time, and even the few who had been in space had limited experience. And certainly none of them had had the extended exposure to space travel this latest endeavor would require. No matter how much time they had spent in simulators.

The notable exceptions to this were most of the bridge personnel, engineering, Robert Porter and, surprisingly, Mrs. Clarice Pickle. It goes without saying that any alien personnel would have had more experience at interstellar travel.

There were two other Earth-born individuals on board with fairly extensive amounts of time logged on starships and they were currently in their quarters in deep discussion with Chief Security Officer Porter.

Robert had reasoned with the Legion for days as to the need to include ND and Stenn on the list of those assigned to the mall starship. He might never had been successful without the staunch support of both Captain Mathews and Clarice Pickle. Since they were the two with the most authority over the ship and the mall, their words carried weight.

ND's quarters occupied a large corner suite at the end of the corridor that gave onto the shuttle bay, leading horizontally from the base of the vertical power shaft that housed the officers' quarters up to the bridge.

"We need to discuss the correlation between several rumors we've heard and intelligence data we have also been able to gather," said ND to Porter and Stenn.

The three were sitting around an eight-foot oval table in a corner of the suite's living room with the readouts from their info ports, or IPs, providing the only light.

Robert Porter spoke in a hushed tone.

"Yes, I have received some disturbing reports myself, and we're going to need to be especially vigilant." He looked particularly concerned as he added, "I don't like hearing the word 'sabotage,' especially when I'm the one responsible for preventing it."

ND continued the conversation along similarly gloomy lines, saying "I'm afraid that even with all of Stenn's resources and skills, he hasn't been able to narrow the possible areas of sabotage down to fewer than four."

"Yes," said Stenn. "Whoever is running this clandestine operation is keeping it very well hidden. But I have been able to determine, with near certainty, that the areas under scrutiny are," he ticked each one off on his fingers: "one, the bridge; two, the shuttle bay; three, the circular plate; and four, the center court in the mall."

"I've never known Stenn to be so inconclusive after so much time spent conducting his investigations," declared N. D. "He has been running down leads since the fifth week of pre-launch." She furrowed her brow, looked at Robert and said, "I had hoped you might contribute some information that would lead us in a more definite direction, but I see that is not to be."

"I wouldn't exactly say I've come here empty-handed!" stated Robert. He went on. "There was one coded communication from somewhere on the moon of Gleb that JA picked up. He said it was directed to the mall storage units. Chief Carter and I were able to partially decipher it. It indicated that the intent of the saboteurs seems to be directed to inflicting not only harm to the ship but violence toward individuals as well. Their aim seems to be to destroy our mission and place the earth in a very tenuous position."

"Were you able to decipher any clues as to their method of accomplishing these goals?" asked Stenn.

Robert shook his head. "We were only able to decipher two sentences and part of a third. It seems that they use several codes within each communication."

Robert stood up and stretched. He was a bit stiff after having been hunched over the table for thirty minutes. He did some bends and twists to work the kinks out. Dressed in the fatigues soldiers wore in field exercises, he smiled down wearily on the two he had become so close to in the last seven years and said, "I don't know about you two, but I need a large cup of strong black coffee."

The bridge of the ship was experiencing a lull in activity. Consequently, the few officers present decided it was time to get clarification on some questions they had for their science officer. Commander Grannison Loche posed the first question.

"How did you go about testing the new Trilliatide propulsion system?" he asked. "I heard that you kind of rubbed it in somebody's face who had particularly criticized you and your team."

Mac hesitated, looking at Ambassador Callurran, who had just entered the bridge. He might take her answer personally.

As he locked eyes with her, he frowned, then smiled and nodded his head at her to indicate he was okay with it.

She began, "As far as the testing was concerned, it was simply a matter of programing some probes to go certain distances and return. Then we would time their flights and evaluate their accuracy. The readings would let us know if the malfunction that had plagued the previous engines was still present."

"How far out did you send the probes?" asked Communications Officer JA Philpot.

"The first two stayed within our solar system. After all, that's where the problem existed in the first place. If those two didn't time out correctly, why try any others?"

Everyone agreed and Mac continued.

"We sent the first prob to Saturn and back. I won't bore you with the exact details, so suffice it to say, in a tad over two hours and forty-six minutes, the probe returned right on time. I can't tell you how excited we were with that result, but we knew we needed more conclusive evidence before we could be certain that we had solved the light speed problem.

"We sent out the second probe to Neptune and the dwarf Pluto. That way we got readings from two separate targets. The results were equally as accurate as the first probe."

She paused and Chief Computer Tech Lindsey Thompson chimed in. "Did you go all the way out to the dwarf planet Eris?" She smiled broadly as she figured she had scored one with the astronomers and physicists there. They knew that space science was not Lindsey's strong suit, but she had been boning up recently.

Mac responded, "Not to the outer reaches of its orbit, but some five point five eight billion miles out. The probe returned in just over sixteen and a half hours."

Keanyn spoke up, "I hope you didn't consider just those two tests as conclusive evidence. I think I know you well enough now to say that there was further testing. You've shown yourself to be quite thorough, and I wouldn't want anything less in my science officer."

He was always trying to set Mac off by poking fun at her, but she never rose to the bait. She just looked at him coolly and a bit condescendingly, as if addressing a misbehaving little boy, and said, "Of course, Captain. We would never think of proclaiming success after such a short trial. In fact, we had to see how the propulsion system would perform in longer tests between solar systems with various heat signatures. We performed several tests to such stars as Alpha Centauri, Sirius, and Tau Ceti to get more accurate and varied test results. Now we were moving from simple light speed to MLS, or multi-light speed. In every test, the probes returned in the exact time!"

She looked over at Keanyn with a superior expression. Then she directed a wide smile to the rest of her audience as they nodded in respectful approval.

Captain Mathews glanced at Mac and became introspective, thinking *I like the tilt of her chin and the gleam in her eyes as she talks about her work.*

Grannison spoke, reminding Mac about the second part of his question. "What about the face rubbing you subjected someone to? I know you're not all business. You are still young and not beyond planning mischief. So how did you do it?"

With another slight nod of her head and brief eye contact with the ambassador, Mac launched into the next part of her narrative.

"There was one particular group of scientists and educators that were quite vocal in their opinions, not only of this project but any other Earth initiatives within the Galactic Legion. None of their opinions were positive or constructive. They even resorted to underhanded political maneuvers and twice to violence in their attempts to thwart the development of the *Cosmic Mall*!"

Mac stopped short of naming the culprit, so Carl Burdgess, the ship's senior navigator, spoke up. "Is the name of this group some kind of top secret?"

Once again, Mac was hesitant to answer. She was spared the embarrassment when Ambassador Yahnsoof Callurran spoke in a clear voice. As a Noradom from Saffo V, his lightly orange-tinted skin and three listening holes on each side of his head made his alien origin clear.

He rose and said, "I believe that Miss Stinson is reluctant to hurt my feelings or embarrass me before you, my colleagues. I assure you that I am not offended nor is my shame the result of anything she is about to recount. So, proceed, my dear, and do so with my full support." He smiled at Mac as he motioned her to continue.

"Yes," she said. "Saffo V was the planet from which most of the trouble came. And while the ambassador was involved in some of the early criticisms, his assignment by the Legion to the earth, and his subsequent friendship with Professor Yargh, changed his viewpoint to a favorable one."

"If I may interrupt, my dear," injected the ambassador. "As I watched you and the rest of your team work so hard to develop the Trilliatide system, I regretted that you hadn't done that sooner and made it your contribution to the Legion.

"But, as we all know," he continued with some sadness in his voice, "once a contribution has been accepted, no other can be substituted for it."

Mac continued in a positive tone. "No regrets, Mr. Ambassador. The *Cosmic Mall* is a refreshing and exciting addition for the Galactic Legion's member planets. Wait till you see the wonderful diversion it will provide for the many inhabitants it will impact at each of its ports-of-call."

"That's right," intoned Lindsey. "I had heard that the Executive Planning Council had been looking for a more light-hearted and entertaining contribution from a planet for some time. So when the earth presented the mall idea, it was just what they had been hoping for."

Grannison looked thoughtful as he said, "I heard that rumor as well but thought it was just a feel-good story to help take the sting out of the copious amounts of criticism we were receiving. How reliable is your information, Lindsey?"

Lindsey pondered, shook her shoulder-length tresses, and replied, "I know I'm a lowly computer tech, but I have an older brother that began serving as an aide to General Beckton shortly after he became a member of the Planning Council and he was privy to a lot of their discussions. He said the subject of a less serious contribution had been mentioned a number of times. I know my brother and he is not given to saying things just to impress someone, and especially not his little sister!"

"That would explain why they gave approval to our contribution so easily," stated Keanyn. He looked over at Mac. "No offense intended toward the honorable ambassador, but you still haven't told us what prank you played on the intellectuals from Saffo V, Mac."

Mac, who was now more relaxed about relaying the tale, began.

"We had one more probe left to send out and hadn't yet decided where to send it. After many suggestions, a member of our team—I won't say who—thought it would be fitting to send it on a one-way trip to Saffo V. Everyone knew the reason behind the suggestion, and since we had all come under attack, both verbally and physically from that direction, there was very little argument against it. In the end we decided that, while our message should be clear, we didn't need to resort to the levels of vitriol—sorry, Mr. Ambassador—they had.

"We programmed the probe to land in the courtyard of the governmental center with a recorded message timed to be played at their upcoming Science and Educational Convention on the evening of the Grand Banquet. The preliminary message was couched in the most inviting and diplomatic tones."

Lindsey shouted, "What happened, Lieutenant. Did you set off some kind of stink bomb or something?"

This prompted a series of snickers, until both Keanyn and Grannison were needed to calm everyone down. Even Ambassador Callurran appeared to be infected by the mirth.

"I will now try to finish my story," said Mac through quiet giggling. "When they were all assembled, the probe's recorder was brought out and placed on a large table in the center of the banquet hall. We had sent a written message within the probe giving the Saffo V dignitaries the impression that the recording was to acknowledge their contribution to the Legion. It did do that, but not in the way they might have expected. When the time arrived, the message began to play automatically. It said, 'Most distinguished members of the scientific, educational, and governmental communities here on Saffo V. The humbled and most appreciative members of the earth team of scientists and educators who have been working diligently on developing a propulsion system for the Legion's starship engines wish to thank you for your tremendous aid in helping us to complete this endeavor. If it had not been for your relentless badgering and vitriolic insults, we may have given up some time ago. Your underhanded attempts to sabotage our work filled us with a fire to succeed. If this is your way of encouraging other Legion planets to succeed then we can say with no doubt in our own case, IT WORKS!'"

Many on the bridge were beginning to chuckle again as Mac came to the climax of her tale.

"'As a final piece of information in which you might be

interested, the probe which carried this recorded message to you, reached you from Earth at the MLS Seven factor without a hitch in the light-speed drive. So, if it's no bother, you might want to check all those equations you said that proved it was impossible to fix that problem. Anyway, keep up the good work of disrespecting everyone's endeavors, whom you believe are inferior. There's no telling how many losers you will encourage to gain new heights and accomplishments . . . Over and above yours, of course! Your most appreciative servants, Earth Scientists.'"

For the sake of Ambassador Callurran, those on the bridge tried valiantly not to give way to the laughter welling up inside them. Most succeeded.

JA Philpot, in an effort to relieve the awkwardness, asked Mac, "How did you know the probe's mission was successful?"

Mac answered, "We had a camera in the recorder programmed to record the entire proceedings, and we also equipped the machine with a fail-safe device to ensure that, once the announcement started, it could not be shut off or turned down. So they got the message!"

Mac's deep auburn hair and her sparkling emerald eyes highlighted her beautiful face that was currently aglow with the joy of the success she had enjoyed since leaving her family farm in the mid-spring of 2213. The success, that she credited more to the help of those around her than to herself, had vaulted her to the top of the Legion's scientific community, so that now, just past her twentieth birthday, she held the respect of the most venerable of scientists and other educators.

Captain Keanyn Mathews was beginning to take note of not only Mac's physical beauty but of her exceptional mental acuity as well.

Grannison Loche had noticed Mac's exceptional qualities from nearly the beginning of their work together on the bridge of the starship. He had often thought that if he ever had a daughter, he would want her to be like Mac.

As life on the bridge of the ship began to get back to the normal business of maneuvering it through the galaxy, Keanyn checked with the various departments to make sure they were ready for the jump to light speed in just twelve more hours.

His first check was with one of his companions from his cadet days, Lieutenant Cheng Wong, who was in charge of the shuttle bay. He was now addressing her on the comm unit and asking, "How are things shaping up down there in the shuttle bay?"

Her reply took him by surprise when she said, "Captain, we just found a crewman badly wounded from what looks like a blow to the head."

"Where did you find him, Cheng?" was Keanyn's quick response.

"In one of the VIP shuttles, sir. He's pretty bad off and is unconscious, but his breathing is strong."

"We both know your skill in patching people up, Lieutenant. So, get him to sick bay and do your stuff."

"I will, Captain," she said as crewmen brought a stretcher to carry the wounded patient away.

"Fine, Cheng, I know he'll get the best care," said Keanyn as he added the thought to himself, *I hope this is just an unfortunate accident and not the result of some attack. That's all we need, an incident before we can even get out of the solar system and get to light speed.*

Chapter 10

The Cosmic Mall

Sitting on her thought-controlled, multi-functional office chair in her suite of rooms on the fourth or mezzanine level of the *Cosmic Mall* was Clarice Pickle. She was trying to hang onto her idea to keep the VIP entourage from their first port-of-call in one group for the grand tour she was planning for them.

Situated in less luxurious chairs around the outer crescent of her spacious half-moon desk were three of her most trusted associates: first assistant to the head of security, Ross Carter; the exceptional investigative agent for undercover ops, Stenn; and her mall manager, Saffaw. *Did I say three trusted associates? Well, Saffaw might be a little less trusted. After all, he is a Wheerie.*

These three had been trying to convince Mrs. Pickle

how potentially dangerous it would be to keep the VIPs together in one group. Ross was saying "The threat of sabotage is very real, ma'am, and one of the main areas of concern is the mall!" The former police commissioner's son continued, "A group of eighteen VIPs could be a tantalizing target for saboteurs wanting to discredit the earth and its contribution."

"Not to mention the amount of time it would take to show just one group the entire mall instead of dividing up the group into three, with six in each," came the statement of the Wheerie, Saffaw, whose animated delivery affected everyone else in the room, including Stenn. He added, "Each group will see a third of the mall, with the entire entourage having seen all of it collectively. Much more efficient and practical."

"Your efficient and practical are always the result of you making more money," chimed in Mrs. Pickle as she scowled at him across the expanse of her lunar-inspired desk. "I do not doubt that you have worked out some way to profit from an arrangement to divide up the VIPs."

Stenn chose this moment to enter the discussion. He got everyone's attention by pitching his voice slightly higher and increasing his normal volume a tad. "Mrs. Pickle, seeing that Mr. Carter has expressed his desire to have three groups instead of one to make it more difficult to focus an attack on the distinguished visitors, and that he virtually echoes the opinions of his boss, Robert Porter, on every occasion that deals with security, my question is, do you not trust the judgment of the head of security for this starship, whose father you hand-picked to head up the security of your fiscal empire on Earth?" He abruptly stopped and fixed a stern stare on the lady sitting directly across from him.

Mrs. Pickle, who was rarely intimidated, fidgeted slightly

in her chair and almost, but not quite, stared directly into Stenn's eyes. She said, "I may have failed to give consideration to that aspect of Mr. Ross' comments, but I do feel that keeping them as one group would make your job of their security easier."

Ross replied gratefully, "While we do appreciate your concern for the difficulty of our job, the main focus for us is on the safety of our visitors. The difficulties we may have to deal with in order to accomplish the security entrusted to us is minor compared to the desired results."

"I appreciate your dedication to your assignment, and with respect to Robert Porter, whose opinion and expertise in these matters I highly regard, I will acquiesce to your wishes to break up the VIPs into three groups," was Clarice Pickle's reply.

With that obstacle now out of the way, they could finalize their plans for the gala tour as it signified the official grand opening of the gargantuan edifice that was the *Cosmic Mall*.

Though the experience of shopping via the mall concept had died out by the mid twenty-first century, circumstances had evolved over the next 150 years that brought the shopping mall back into vogue.

As the mall concept was dying out, the computer-generated, online shopping became "the way" to conduct consumer purchasing. Over time, corruption crept in as retail suppliers and manufacturers substituted inferior products for the quality goods ordered by consumers. It finally became necessary for the governments to enact laws and provide strict oversight of the online retail domain. While this resulted in quality merchandise as ordered, the selection and style of products lessened.

Another factor was that the social aspect of the

shopping experience had been eliminated, and in time, many began yearning for that again. The result of all this was a renewing of the entrepreneurial spirit. People were now venturing into retail on a more personal and individual level. This started with the small individually owned or family-operated business and grew to a more corporate level by the late twenty-second century.

Clarice Pickle was at the forefront of a new phase of consumer retail marketing. She continued to be a visionary in the field and was a major proponent of the *Cosmic Mall* as Earth's contribution to the Legion. One of the major reasons for the acceptance of the mall contribution was her huge popularity and success (not to mention her vast fortune) in this area. In fact, she conducted a two-hour lecture for the people, both earthen and alien, who made up the managers and employees of the mall as part of a training seminar to introduce them to this brand-new experience in consumer retail. Visionary and new, though it may seem, it is actually a classic case of "what goes around comes around."

After another two hours of discussing the final arrangements for the VIP tour, the four individuals exited Mrs. Pickle's office onto a panoramic viewing platform that gave a magnificent oversight of the *Cosmic Mall*. The mezzanine was actually an extension of the mall's third level on the port side of the starship. It housed not only Clarice's office but her lavish stateroom, lounge and reception area, a conference room, and library. The viewing platform allowed Clarice to provide her guests an eye-popping opportunity to see her grand edifice in all its glory.

"Grand" is certainly the correct word with 212 retail establishments on each of three main levels; the mall was nearly a mile long.

But as large as the "mall" was, it was only a part of the structure of the main fuselage.

The main fuselage of the ship was cylindrical, with a slight tapering at each end. It housed eight levels of various lengths and heights within a rectangular structure. The top three levels contained the mall.

The next two, rooming for mall employees. The sixth level contained engineering and quarters for the engineering crew. In levels seven and eight were found the nerve center of the starship. It's engines and the main frame of the entire computer system, controlling virtually every function, from climate control to the defensive shields and key engine functions.

Protruding from each side of the fuselage from two-thirds aft, extending some fifty feet beyond the fuselage, were the massive, main thrust engines. This is where the Trilliatide light-speed engines were housed. As Chief Davis had mentioned in his description of his first view of the starship, it was both odd and awe-inspiring at the same time.

Concerning the four individuals standing on the viewing deck, it was Saffaw who spoke first saying "This must be the sixth or seventh time I've been up here and it's as if I'm seeing the mall for the first time. It is magnificent."

In this moment of complete candor, Clarice responded, "Though I question your sincerity frequently, this is not an occasion in which I do so. Thank you, Saffaw." She then looked off in the distance as though seeing a vision and said, "I feel exactly the same every time I come here as well."

The other two, Stenn and Ross, said nothing, but their faces reflected similar feelings. Which was saying a lot for the often-stoic Stenn.

Every level was anchored on each end by two large retailers. Approximately at the center of each level were somewhat smaller anchor stores on each side of the mall's central concourse that contained both regular walkways and moving walkways. Other modes of transport included self-programmed transit pods that took shoppers only to those establishments they had programmed into the pod.

There were many Earth-based retailers occupying the mall. In fact, 45 percent of the stores were from the earth. The remaining percentage were from the far flung reaches of the galaxy. Some examples included the aforementioned Moolyn Jal bead chain from the planet Garsden, the Panto Brothers from Krolmaton, whose line of sweet meats included the tempting chocolate-like, strawberry cream-filled, and mint-glazed bon-bon-style "freemers," a delicacy from the Setto region of Krolmaton. Of course, the flavors just described are Earth equivalents. The actual names and the by-products from which they derive are quite alien.

As far as Jal beads are concerned, they are stones crafted from a substance known as "valcys" that grows wild in a small valley in the southern hemisphere of Garsden. When the valcys is picked at its prime ripeness, a central seed in its core is extracted and molded into a multi-hued stone about the size of a pearl. A peculiar quality of this stone is that each of its seven colors can be extracted from it by means of a process known only to a family of ancient descent from the small valley where the valcys originates. The secret is passed down through the generations and only the current matriarch is entrusted with its safekeeping.

One in every 122 seeds from the valcys has a plain, non-colored stone, and it is into one of these that one of the seven extracted colors is placed. This makes a single-colored Jal bead one hundred times more expensive than the more vibrant multi-colored ones.

Other alien-based retailers ranged from out-of-this-world (literally) fashion designs to some of the most bizarre and beautiful all-terrain vehicles, with modes of propulsion ranging from hover craft to dune burrowing forward and reverse drills (you'd have to see it to understand it).

With such a variety of known and unknown commodities displayed in any form of recognizable and not so recognizable ways, the *Cosmic Mall* was a magnificent feast for the eyes.

Perhaps the most incredible display of all was to be found at the mall's central court.

In the three-tiered central court of the *Cosmic Mall,* a galaxy full of wonders could be experienced. The single feature of all three tiers was the 140-foot-high and fifty-foot-wide waterfall that cascaded into an iridescent pool of Jal bead-infused water. To keep the deafening sound of the water from being a distraction to the other features in the central court, it was enclosed within a tube of clear plydacene, a strong plastic-like substance that was also used as a sound inhibitor.

The food court was found on the first level. But a food court like no other as it featured six restaurants of Earth cuisine and eighteen others that ranged from the gourmet creations of the Alpha Centauri sector to the spice-crazed delicacies of the Gullroodites and Sharlees. Not to be overlooked was the Raushdonian pub from the home world of Saffaw. Among its offerings was a twelve-ingredient drink called "Drishkt." It was challenged that no earthling could remain standing after more than two swallows. That myth was firmly debunked when Tom Palmer didn't fall flat on his face until *after* the third swallow.

Another feature of the first level was a grand center stage bordered by the twenty-four restaurants. Just in front of the eating establishments were rows of chairs that would rise from the floor as the restaurants receded. Add to that the number of people that could watch from their tables in the eateries and well over three thousand humans, humanoids, and others could enjoy the variety of acts displayed daily on the stage.

The acts ranged from plays and musicals to bands of all kinds, single performers, and circus style acts. There was also a night devoted to anyone who wanted to showcase their talent or lack thereof.

Needless to say, this night was always the night when the Raushdonian pub had the most customers and best sales. That's not to say that there were never any truly talented performers on those nights. Some were invited back to perform on regular nights, and one or two who were tourists and visitors went back to their planet and became famous entertainers.

Other features of the central court included a Realism Theater. This attraction made it possible for as many as six people at a time to program a selected scene from literature, history, or their own imagination, enter a thirty-by-forty-five-foot room and experience that scene as if they were there. Of course, if any scene threatened any imaginary harm to the customer, the computers either ended the scene or altered the action. It goes without saying that multiple disclaimers and restrictions were given before anyone used the attraction.

In addition to the individual rooms, there was a large sixty-by-eighty-foot auditorium where groups of twelve to twenty people could experience an ensemble adventure.

The Realism Theater occupied the bulk of the second level of the center court, which also featured an interactive exhibit of certain aspects of the bridge of the Starship

Cosmic Mall. In addition, a "small" snack kiosk that had a bar, seating sixteen individuals of earthly and alien size—plus six tables with six chairs each—was available on this level. The name of the kiosk was the Sixer Club.

The third level of the center court contained the most unusual natural feature of the mall. Under the direction of the two botany scientists, Doctors Stella Steel and Larindo kwark, was the dome covered Interstellar Botanical Gardens.

Packed within the three point six acres of the gardens were some of the most exotic plants to be found in all of the Galactic Legion's territory. Visitors could walk along loam-covered and rock-bordered pathways to the sights, smells, and sounds of an exotic rainforest. The serpentine pathway would enter the plydacene barrier where you could feel and hear the full power of the waterfall feature. In fact, they could even walk behind it through a cavern-like portal. Upon exiting the gardens, visitors were treated to some of the most delectable fruits and fruit dishes and drinks to be found in the galaxy.

To describe even in the briefest of details, the remaining wonders of the *Cosmic Mall* would fill enough pages for a book. The mall from which the starship derived its name was indeed out of this world!

One thing that needs to be mentioned at this point has to do with time. With the presence of a retail establishment, there must be opening and closing times, shift changes, lunch breaks, etc. This begs the question, on what basis are days, hours, and minutes measured? The answer involves two standards of measuring time.

As the Galactic Legion grew, some form of time standardization needed to be developed. Since space-travel time was shared by all the races who used it, a standard star time (SST) was developed. The dating was a formula drawn from the main influences of the speed of light and the expansion rate of the universe among other minor ingredients. The bigger problem had to do with the time keeping of each of the individual planets that made up the members of the Galactic Legion.

Most of the inhabitants of the member planets wanted to keep their own forms of time keeping based on their planet's distance from its star and the time each took to rotate on its axis just as Earth time is measured. There were some that had twenty-four-hour cycles but most varied one way or the other. For instance, the planet Sarkof is 165 million miles from its sun and rotates every thirty-nine hours, made up of seventy-five minutes each, on its axis. This makes their day divided into two halves of nineteen hours each, with a zero hour marking the exact middle of a day.

Another example is the planet of Zisk, which is only about 60 percent the size of Earth and is a mere fifty-eight million miles from its sun. Its rotation on its axis takes only eighteen hours of forty-eight minutes each, so that the inhabitants only have the Earth equivalent of seven hours and twelve minutes of daylight each day. "Make hay while the sun shines" really means something there.

With all this being the case, the Legion's ruling council decided to use SST to gauge space-time travel and distance only. This standard was incorporated into the MLS, or multi-light-speed, calculations from MLS-1 to MLS-9 which is astronomically greater than the speed of light.

On their home world and within the confines of their own starships, time is kept according to their planetary clocks.

That is why the *Cosmic Mall's* hours were counted according to Earth time.

The four people on the observation platform were not

thinking about any of these details at that particular moment. Mrs. Pickle was trying to figure out the seating arrangements for the eighteen dignitaries from the Eridean star system that would constitute their first official port of call.

Ross Carter was mulling over the manpower needed to provide protection for the visiting dignitaries, not to mention the regular security details for the everyday shoppers. *I'm going to have to go over some more changes in the arrangements we've made with Saffaw,* he thought.

Saffaw's thoughts were not along those same lines, though. He was mentally rechecking his figures on some recent "arrangements" he had worked out with some suppliers from Obnesia in the Keplar-47 star system.

What occupied Stenn's thoughts was much more ominous. He was still bothered by the fact that he couldn't narrow down the possible areas of sabotage to less than three. He had been able to eliminate the bridge as a possibility when he found out that the aim of the saboteurs was not the command staff or even any other influential member of the starship. They wanted to do damage to a sector of the ship that would impact the visiting dignitaries. In that way, they could do the most harm to the earth and its mission.

"We could probably stay here all day," said Clarice. "I'm certain we all have too much on our plates in preparation for our docking at Drathon Three Eridea than to hang about here, as pleasant as it is."

Ross was the first to respond. "Most assuredly, Mrs. Pickle." He continued, "I actually need to speak to Saffaw concerning some necessary changes I have just thought of that will be vital for this first visit."

Saffaw's reply showed his frustration with what he perceived were more endless details. "Really, Mr. Carter, didn't we just strain out every possible event that could occur during the upcoming tour? Does your mind—not to mention that of your boss, Mr. Porter—never take a break from security matters?"

"When you have an event of this magnitude and importance, and your responsibility is the safety and well-being of hundreds, if not thousands, of people, it must constantly be a consideration of your entire thought process. Add to that the fact that this kind of event has never been undertaken in the history of the Galactic Legion, and I think you get where I am coming from," was Ross Carter's emphatic reply.

For once Saffaw was thoroughly embarrassed, chastised, and speechless. Clarice exclaimed, "I do believe that you have performed the impossible, Mr. Carter. You have humbled Saffaw and shut his mouth at the same time."

Saffaw recovered quickly and said, "Not at all, Mrs. Pickle. While I do indeed appreciate the appropriate seriousness with which Mr. Carter takes his responsibility, I was not making light of the gravity of the situation but was merely concerned that his commendable sense of responsibility for his duties and laudable dedication to this project might cause him some undo anxiety which might affect his health. And it was for those reasons that I voiced my concern."

Clarice Pickle's reply to this was to throw her hands in the air and declare, "I hope you gentlemen can now see what utter ridiculousness I must put up with on a daily basis from this scamp. If he wasn't so effective in what I hired him to do, I would have sacked him before we ever boarded this ship!"

Stenn broke in before it turned into the regular back and forth of "he said, she said" that these two antagonists were known for by saying "If you will pardon me, Mrs. Pickle, as has been noted, we all have much we need to attend to." He continued, "As for myself, I need to consult with my mother and Mr. Porter about further countermeasures concerning the possible sabotage."

And with that they all said their goodbyes, wishing each other success in their endeavors.

Chapter 11

Light Speed

"What was a crewman doing in a VIP shuttle in the first place?" asked Captain Keanyn Mathews, concerning the injured crewman that was found unconscious in the shuttle bay and was now in sick bay. The reply from Chief Donnard, head of the security patrol that had discovered the victim, was not in direct connection to the question but got everyone's attention nonetheless.

"He's not actually a crewman, sir. At least, not a crewman from this vessel," said the chief. "I looked for his ID but couldn't find anything but a small wristband with the name Salfrod on it. We have no one by that name listed on the roster sheet for this ship's crew."

Lieutenant Cheng Wong spoke up. "That means he's probably a—"

"Stowaway!" interrupted the captain.

The ship's doctor, Alfred Karushkin, leaned into the conversation and noted, "Gentlemen, and ladies, the status of *my patient's* assignment to a particular vessel, as relevant as it may be to you, carries little weight in the sick bay where I am trying to monitor and treat his injuries so that at *the appropriate time,* he will be able to answer your questions as to his presence on this ship. As you are currently in my domain, I am telling you that if your inquiries do not consist solely of the medical status of this patient, I will be forced to ask you to leave!"

"Is he always this protective of his territory?" whispered Edward Butler into Cheng's ear. Edward had just arrived in sick bay in time to hear the doctor's retort to Keanyn.

Cheng whispered back, "Not usually, but the good doctor likes to remind the captain, on occasion, who's in charge when it comes to sick bay. It's all done lightheartedly." She tilted her head in the doctor's direction so that Edward could take note of his mischievous smile.

"I stand corrected, my good doctor," stated Keanyn with a similar grin on his face. He did continue, though, by saying "I am concerned about the patient's health, therefore, may I inquire as to your estimate of his recovery time?"

The doctor replied with a more serious demeanor. "Your question is valid, Captain." He began to explain, "The patient, let's call him Salfrod, is a Cherillian. You can tell due to the fact that his wide nose has a third nostril with an extremely enhanced olfactory gland. This feature does enhance his sense of smell, especially as it increases his ability to detect any odor that serves as food for him. He can particularly detect plant and soil odors. A decided advantage since they are strictly vegetarians." The doctor had reverted to his medical school instructor mode during the mini lecture on Cherillians.

His audience had seemed to be riveted to his speech when Edward Butler said, "I'm sorry to interrupt, but I came here to get something for this headache I have."

"No reason to apologize, Mr. Butler," answered Alfred Karushkin. "This is a sick bay with a dispensary at your disposal."

"Besides," chimed in the captain, "I left your brother in command, and his shift will be over when I get back. I will leave it to you to brief him on this situation when he gets back to your quarters before you come on for your shift and the jump to light speed." Keanyn paused and looked quizzically at Edward Butler and said, "I was surprised when he gave that privilege to you as his younger brother."

Edward replied, "That's because if anything goes wrong, I'll get the blame, not him."

Everyone chuckled quietly at this retort, knowing how famous the banter was between the two brothers even when they weren't in the same room together.

Edward said, "I will be sure to pass on any pertinent information to Grann—oh, I mean Commander Loche—as soon as I return to our quarters, sir."

"Make sure you do," was the captain's response. He then turned his attention back to the doctor and said, "I would greatly appreciate it if you would inform me as soon as Salfrod is capable of receiving visitors, Doctor. I believe our knowledgeable liaison officer, Ambassador Callurran, is quite fluent in several Cherillian dialects and I would like some answers."

"I will be certain to inform you of the patient's condition to receive visitors as soon as I know it myself," said the doctor. "The medical staff is fully aware of the serious possibilities concerning this incident. While we are primarily interested in his recovery, we are also a part of this starship's mission and are keenly concerned with its success. Anything we can do to ensure that nothing threatens that success, we will do."

"I deeply appreciate your sincere statement of cooperation, Dr. Karushkin." Captain Mathew's grateful words were accompanied by a broad smile and a firm handshake.

Everyone left sick bay except Edward Butler who still needed something for his headache. As he and the doctor walked to the dispensary, Edward asked Dr. Karushkin if the Cherillian patient would be able to account for his presence even if he regained consciousness.

"I have heard that his head wound was fairly severe, with the possibility that there may be permanent brain damage."

"You seem to be well-informed for someone not connected to the medical or shuttle bay staffs, who've had the most exposure to Mr. Salfrod," was the doctor's reply.

Edward blushed slightly at Karushkin's somewhat disciplinary tone but quickly recovered and said, "You can never discount the rumor mill, Doctor, and this incident has caused much concern and conversation. And while I don't usually put much credence in gossip, I have the highest regard for Lieutenant Wong. I was on the bridge when she made her report to Captain Mathews."

"I see," said the doctor and continued, "I know this kind of speculation can't be helped in such a situation just as we are preparing to jump to light speed. But it needs to be kept in check as much as possible."

"I couldn't agree with you more, sir, and that is why I waited until I could speak with you alone and either put proof to the rumors or discard them completely," Edward said. "I don't really have a headache. That was just an excuse to talk with you."

The doctor smiled. "I rather thought that might be the

case, Mr. Butler. You showed no real signs of having a headache. Your eyes were not squinting into the rather bright light of the sick bay, and you showed no other facial signs that usually accompany a headache requiring even mild medication. Really, you need to bone up on your acting skills. Pun intended."

They both smiled as Dr. Karushkin closed the door to the dispensary behind them so that they wouldn't be disturbed during their discussion.

The bridge was in a state of controlled frenzy as everyone was making their last-minute settings and adjustments for the jump to MLS. The engineering deck was also buzzing with the same high degree of activity. Surprisingly, two of the people whom you would think to be among the busiest were calmly sitting at their posts, taking stock of all the ant-like industriousness going on around them.

Captain Keanyn Mathews and Head Science Officer McCardle Stinson quietly but intently observed how all of the frenetic energy was being translated into the precise calculations needed for this historic event. Everyone was making absolutely certain that the figures and formulas they were responsible for were exact and in proper working order. As far as it depended on them, when the "good to go" was given, it would be 100 percent certain.

When he was completely satisfied that all systems were ready, the captain rose from his command seat and signaled for attention. He addressed the bridge crew in a cheerful and confident voice.

"Before I invite the observers onto the bridge, I want to extend a warm and sincere thank you to each and every one of you for all of your hard work and diligence in making this moment possible. That is why I wanted even the off-duty personnel to be here for the historic launching of the first Earth-built space vessel to achieve light speed." He paused at this point, and with shining proud eyes, raised his voice up a level and continued, "Yes! Even multi-light-speed!"

The crew erupted in a shout of victory.

When Keanyn had quieted them down, he turned to the communications officer and said, "Mr. Philpot, key in the comm unit to allow our observers on Earth to be a part of this momentous occasion."

"Aye, sir. Ship-wide communications and the line to Earth are on and receiving our distinguished guests for this noteworthy event," came the response from Communications Officer Jonas Alexander Philpot.

Captain Mathews directed a mischievous grin and wink in the direction of the communications officer, and it was returned in kind by JA along with a salute.

The "distinguished" guests included General Anthony Beckton, Dr. Carlotta Simmons, and Grand Admiral Haffen Hoo Wangrung. Among the observers from the ship were Ambassador Yhansoof Callurran, Dr. Alfred Karushkin, Chief of Security Robert Porter, Mrs. Clarice Pickle, and Stenn. Stenn's mother, ND, had been invited but declined, saying "It is not in my nature to make overt and often insincere congratulatory gestures. I am certain we will achieve light speed, and MLS for that matter, and you won't need me to accomplish it."

With everyone in place, Keanyn stood in front of the commander's console and addressed the crowd. "Ladies and gentlemen, distinguished officers, diplomats, and professionals. We are about to witness, and for some of us, experience, a greatly historic event. In less time than it will take me to say all of this, we will enter the realm of faster-than-light speed and be as far from the earth as it has taken us two and one-half days to accomplish." He acknowledged the equal amounts of polite applause and quiet laughter before adding "Of course, many of us have already traveled at MLS, not just light speed. But NONE OF US have ever done so on a completely engineered and constructed EARTH VESSEL!"

The ovation from both the starship and the planet was deafening and lasted several minutes. When it had subsided, he got their attention by saying "Therefore, when I give the command, we will travel through MLS Three, then Five, and reach our cruising speed of six thousand eight hundred and forty-six times the speed of light, or MLS Seven. We will arrive at our first port-of-call, Drathon Three Eridea, in just one week." With a determined gesture toward both his pilot and navigator, he said, "Mr. Burdgess and Mr. Butler, is the course plotted and the helm responsive?"

"Aye, Captain" was their simultaneous reply. With that, the captain addressed engineering, "Then, Stokes, let's turn the lights on!"

The engineer's reply was "We're flipping the switch right now, sir!"

Mac stood in the vertical power lift with the captain, looking at him with inquisitive eyes and said, "Where did you get all of that charisma with your oratory skills, sir?" As she finished the question, she looked at Keanyn with a tilt of her head that he found attractive.

"Really, Officer Stinson? That is the kind of ability one in your position should assume the commander of a starship must possess," he chastised her in mock severity.

Mac's response was to put on an air of sensitivity and

whine, "That hurts me deeply, Captain. To think that I should assume anything about a superior officer after all we've been through together."

"Don't you mean, after all you've put me through?" came Captain Mathews' retort.

Mac's auburn hair fell in soft ringlets around her smooth, oval face with sparkling emerald eyes and glistening full lips. She again gave that tilt of her head. *To have all of that intelligence wrapped up in such a beautiful package is so unfair to other women,* thought Keanyn as the lift began to slow on its approach to the bottom level that gave onto the long corridor leading to the main fuselage of the ship. His thoughts were interrupted by Mac's reply.

"What I've put you through?" was her incredulous response. "Permission to speak freely, sir."

Keanyn said, "Permission granted."

Mac swallowed nervously and said, "Your never-ending practical jokes are torture since they are neither funny nor make any point other than the fact that you don't have a clue!"

"Duly noted, Science Officer." Anything else Keanyn might have said in return was never uttered due to the fact that as soon as the lift doors opened, they were approached by an excited Lieutenant Cheng Wong.

"Do you have some information for us, Cheng?" questioned the captain.

Her energy, coupled with a graceful elegance, made her the perfect commander of the shuttle bay. A position on this starship that was highly important. Her excellent observation skills insured that very little got past Cheng Wong. She stated, "I've just received some information, Captain, that could shed some light on our stowaway's reasons for being on this ship. Could we go somewhere more private to talk, sir?"

"Seeing that almost everyone is either on the bridge or

in the mall, any quarters in this corridor will suffice," offered Mac.

They found the third crew's quarters to be open and unoccupied. After finding some seats, the captain turned to Cheng and said, "While I have always had good reason to trust your sources and their information, this situation is so critical that I need to be really certain about what you will tell me, Cheng. I hope you don't mind."

"Certainly not, Captain," said Cheng. "In fact, I'd have been surprised if you hadn't asked for my sources. To that point, sir, I know that Science Officer Stinson is a member of your trusted bridge staff, but do you want her knowing information this delicate? It's not that I don't trust her, and it's obvious that you do, but this is one of those need-to-know situations."

"I can clear this up with one statement, Lieutenant Wong," Keanyn said rather abruptly. Then he smiled apologetically and said more softly, "Sorry, Lieutenant, but I have now worked very closely with our head science officer for better than three months and she has proven many times over how trustworthy she can be. Not unlike some other young lady I worked very closely with some three years ago and who I literally trusted with my life."

Cheng Wong was blushing profusely from that comment. Not from chastisement but from the personal knowledge about the subject of his reference. "I couldn't understand better, sir," she acknowledged.

Captain Mathews dissipated the awkward moment by his next statement. "Are you going to sit there and blush all day, or are we going to hear this big news of yours?"

Cheng rousted herself and sat up more straightly, saying "While our stowaway may be a Cherillian, he made a stopover on Saffo V—ostensibly for fuel and supplies that would normally take a few hours, not three days—and when he left, he had his ship brought over to Ambassador Callurran's launch pad."

"That raises some very interesting and disturbing questions, Lieutenant," Keanyn responded. He took a moment to think about the implications of Cheng's statement and added, "We don't want to jump to the wrong conclusion, though. This could be a move employed by another party to direct our attentions to the wrong person or persons." He looked worried.

Mac, who had purposely remained in the background, scooted forward in her chair and fixed her gaze on the other two, saying "I agree, Captain, but it must be noted that Ambassador Callurran had been a mild dissenter of this project in the beginning, and by seemingly making the switch to our support and obtaining a trusted and highly influential posting on this vessel, he is in an excellent position to receive and dispense very sensitive information."

"That was my thought as well," remarked Cheng and continued, "and his initial dissension may have been more than mild. He could have feigned his change of opinion in order to get the kind of assignment he has indeed received."

Keanyn scratched his chin as he considered this possibility. He shook his head as if to deny the validity of this shocking premise and added, "While I do acknowledge the definite possibility of that being the case and certainly worth investigating, I am inclined toward giving the ambassador the benefit of the doubt for the time being." He continued as he became more absorbed in the mystery that was unfolding, "Does Robert Porter know about this?" He looked keenly at Cheng Wong as he posed this question, and she responded instantly.

"I dispatched my most-trusted aid to locate him and

inform him as I deduced that this information was too delicate for anything less than face-to-face communication."

"Smart thinking, Lieutenant" was the captain's response. "In addition, I would like the three of us to meet with him ASAP!"

"Do you think there is anyone else we should include in this 'brain trust,'" added the head science officer. "While I understand that we want to keep the number of this group to a minimum for security purposes, there are some very skilled individuals on this ship whose talent and know-how would be invaluable." She quickly interjected, "Stenn and his mother, for example."

"You took the words right out of my mouth, Mac. And I would add one more," said Keanyn.

Mac replied, "Are you thinking of someone else in the security field?"

Keanyn had a conspiratorial look as he revealed who he thought this final member of their investigative ensemble should be. "I have been closely observing this person's actions and deciphering his ability to solve problems, and I feel that my second-in-command, Grannison Loche, would make a solid addition to our group. Not to mention that his first-rate piloting skills would come in handy."

Cheng added the amused statement, "His physical attributes could also give us the 'muscle' we might need if—no—*when* we find ourselves in a sticky situation."

"You've known our captain longer than I have, Cheng, but I've seen his penchant for finding trouble as well," stated Mac.

"Oh, I've not only seen it, ma'am, but I've been in the thick of it on many occasions," said the shuttle-bay commander with a wide smile.

"All right, you two! Remember where and who you are,"

came the resounding voice of Captain Keanyn Mathews. I'm all for a little joking among friends, but we are officers in a highly important and dangerous mission, and we should act like it!"

The two female officers acknowledged, "Aye-aye, sir!"

To soften the blow, Keanyn said, "Sometimes in stressful situations we feel the need to lessen that stress with humor. Add to that the fact that we are still quite young and have some maturing to do. Notice, I said 'we.'"

Mac said, "Thank you, sir. Your comments are another reason why they chose the right person to captain the mall starship."

As they were walking back up the corridor to the power lift, Keanyn said to Mac and Cheng, "Head Science Officer Stinson, see about recruiting Commander Loche. I happen to know that he thinks a lot of you and considers you as the daughter he never had. Your words will carry a lot of weight with him.

"And Lieutenant Wong, you seem to have caught Stenn's ear in this latest development, so I think he would put stock in your words." If he sees the need to join our investigative team then his mother and Mr. Porter won't be hard to convince."

Their replies were in the affirmative and all three shook hands as they reached the power lift. Cheng reversed her direction to head back to her position on the shuttle deck. Mac would take the power lift all the way to the bridge where there was a full laboratory in quarters, situated behind the bridge where she often went to work and think. The Captain would got to his quarters one level below the bridge to do some deep thinking on their course moving forward.

Chapter 12

The Stowaway

Two days later, the Sabotage Investigative Team was assembled in the captain's quarters. They were sitting in business chairs brought in by Keanyn from the conference chamber for visiting dignitaries. Since they wouldn't be in use for at least another five days, he didn't see the harm in using them now.

They weren't as easy to obtain as he thought. It seems that they were under the supervision of Robert Porter's second-in-command, Ross Carter—and Lieutenant Carter took his responsibility quite seriously. He had allocated those chairs for the visiting aliens (at least those in humanoid form) and that is where they would remain.

Keanyn spoke to Robert as he entered the room. "Lieutenant Carter is not the laid-back, fun-loving guy I knew him to be at the academy, and I was counting on our past history to facilitate the ease with which I could obtain these chairs. What have you done to him?"

A cunning smile appeared on Robert's face as he answered the captain's question. "The nature of security alone can sober one's attitude, Captain, but Ross has also had to spend a lot of time dealing with Saffaw and all of the pre-visit details. I am sure you know how frustrating any prolonged time spent with our loquacious mall manager can be."

The captain just nodded his head.

Robert furthered his narrative, saying "While the lieutenant had his own mischievous nature, it was no match for Saffaw's antics, and Lieutenant Carter saw the need to rearrange his own attitude toward seriousness and has developed a keen aptitude for his responsibilities as my assistant."

Robert Porter's visage was calm and just a bit smug as he folded his hands across his chest and settled more comfortably into one of the aforementioned seven chairs. A brief sigh escaped his lips as he concluded by saying "Lieutenant Carter is still a bit playful, but he demonstrates it in a more subtle manner."

Keanyn said, "I'm sure that learning that lesson was not an accident. It seems that a subtle playfulness is required by many in the field of security, even one's superiors."

"You did ask, Captain. I was just answering your question," came Robert Porter's reply.

"And I thank you for that answer, Mr. Porter," said Keanyn, adding "I know now to be more cautious around you in the future."

Everyone at the table had an expression of amusement as the discussion came to an end. Of all in attendance, ND surprisingly made the final comment, saying "You should have come to me first, Captain. I have had the experience of several years of Mr. Porter's subtleties and could have clued you in on his sense of humor."

As the meeting unfolded, it was made certain that all were aware of the latest information concerning the stowaway and his visit to Saffo V.

Stenn was the first to comment. "I know you have considered the possibility of the use of Ambassador Callurran's launch pad as a ruse to throw suspicion in his direction and away from another area, but this development helps me to add a piece of disjointed knowledge I had received to fit this puzzle we are considering."

Cheng sounded concerned as she said, "Do you mean that your information will confirm the ambassador's involvement?"

"Not absolutely confirm. But it is certainly damning" was Stenn's reply.

Keanyn made the next statement. "Well, let's have it then, Stenn."

"Two days before our pal Salfrod blasted off from Ambassador Callurran's launch pad, he was heard communicating with the ambassador. Then, shortly after this, Callurran allocated some extra fuel for Salfrod's fuel cells. I obtained a copy of the requisition form with the ambassador's signature. While this was curious information, it could have been just a matter of simple protocol that required Callurran's signature. That's how we obtained the requisition form. We have been monitoring all of the ship's communications to and from any of the home worlds represented here, and the requisition was just part of that operation. As I said, it was just a disjointed piece of info that was a bit curious until we identified the stowaway, and, as we've just learned Salfrod's ship actually launched from the ambassador's pad, it makes that communication much more interesting."

Everyone looked deeply concerned as they processed this information. Ambassador Yhansoof Callurran had become an integral and well-liked member of the crew of the mall starship. No one wanted to think of him as a master conspirator against the ship's mission.

Mac put voice to these feelings. "I know that the ambassador initially was vocal in his reluctance to accept our contribution to the Legion, and he expressed his strong doubts that the earth was worthy of becoming a member, as do you all. But his close association with a number of Earth representatives after he had made those early comments, not to mention my own close association with him ever since we boarded the ship, makes me have serious reservations as to his direct involvement in any sabotage conspiracy."

ND expressed her thoughts.

"We know how you have come to trust Ambassador Callurran and his loyalty, Mac, and it is a credit to your character. But having spent years in the security and espionage field, Mr. Porter, my son, and I have seen too many individuals whose acting skills could con the keenest minds into giving up valuable information. Some of these con artists are so good, that the person they are conning doesn't even know he is divulging the information. Therefore, we have to remain skeptical and—yes—cynical."

Grannison Loche next contributed to the discussion. "It seems that we will need to arrive at a compromise concerning the ambassador until we can uncover enough evidence to make a definitive decision. I, for one, am willing to keep all the options open."

"That is a very intelligent statement, Commander Loche," Keanyn observed as he leaned forward in his chair. He continued, "We can't be making snap judgments. We all have valuable observations to make, and we may find that one or two of us may know something that will turn our investigation in the right direction." He sat back and made an open-handed gesture to indicate that the floor was open for additional comments.

Robert Porter was the next to speak.

"Since we only have five days before our first visitors come aboard, we need to formulate the steps to take and the expediency with which we need to carry them out. For instance, do we know all the details concerning Salfrod's insistence on leaving from Ambassador Callurran's launch pad? Also, we need to question the ambassador about his knowledge of the use of his pad by a now-known stowaway."

Cheng chimed in with, "We shouldn't need to worry about that arousing his suspicions, that we are focusing on him as a prime suspect, since it would be logical for security to approach him because of the circumstances. We don't want to spook him into covering his tracks and making our job that much harder."

Stenn finally added his contribution by saying "I can certainly dig into the reasons for Salfrod's actions on Saffo V. In fact, I've already started—if the rest of you don't mind?"

"Of course not," remarked the captain. "I would have suggested you as the one for the job in the first place. Are there any other suggestions you would like to put forward?" He scanned the six other chairs for volunteers.

ND motioned that she would like to speak. "Have we forgotten the fact that our stowaway was viciously attacked?

If it had been a member of this crew who wanted to protect the ship and its mission from an intruder, he or she would have remained in the shuttle to report the details and not run away. That, of course, suggests that the stowaway has an accomplice on the ship who may very well be Ambassador Callurran. The fact that all of the security scanners, both video and psychological, had been turned off in that shuttle suggests a certain knowledge of the system not everyone has. Indeed, we need to find out if the ambassador has that training or not. It could either eliminate him as a suspect or add the worrisome detail that there is yet another accomplice on board."

She had that knowing smile on her face when the in-ship comm came on, and Comms Officer Philpot announced, "Captain Mathews, you're needed in sick bay. The stowaway is awake."

Keanyn quickly turned to the rest of the room's occupants and assigned them duties. "Stenn, you may continue with your inquiries on Saffo V you've already begun. ND, would you mind conducting a subtle but thorough interview of Ambassador Callurran, which I know is a particular skill of yours?"

Her reply was "I would have been insulted if you had assigned anyone else to that responsibility. The ambassador and I have had a number of occasions to engage in deep conversation and, often times, over a meal or coffee and dessert. I think the latter would be more suitable on this occasion. That would give it a more casual air and perhaps keep his defenses down."

As she made these comments, ND was softly stroking her lengthy black and gold tresses with a conspiratorial gleam in her very dark blue eyes. If asked, no man would ever have guessed her age any closer than fifteen to twenty years in either direction. But they certainly would have to acknowledge her eloquence and beauty.

On this occasion, no one in the room had any time or inclination to consider such a pleasant past time as they were all caught up in the moment and the duties at hand. The captain continued to make assignments.

"Lieutenant Wong, I would like you to thoroughly reexamine the vids of any activity around that shuttle, both before and immediately after the discovery of our stowaway. You might also question any individuals who may have been anywhere near it during that time."

Cheng said, "I get your drift, sir, and while I've already done some of that, I'm sure I can be more thorough."

"Good. I think that since we now have a more definite goal in mind, we can all be more thorough in our investigation." Keanyn paused as he turned to take in the three others who had yet to be given an assignment. His voice sounded confident as he said, "Mr. Porter, Science Officer Stinson, and Commander Loche, if you would do me the pleasure of accompanying me as we interview our uninvited guest. I would value your observations."

This comment brought about the conclusion of their meeting, and as Keanyn and his three companions walked toward sick bay, Robert Porter turned to the captain and said, "My compliments, sir, that was masterfully done. If you weren't already the captain, I'd be in fear for my job."

"No worries there, Commander," came Keanyn's reply. He continued, "I am going to especially need your insight and expertise on this interview. I'm certain you'll be able to pick up on subtle clues Salfrod may supply in our conversation with him. I doubt that I would be near as adept as you in that regard."

Robert Porter smiled a little as he answered by saying

"That's as may be, sir, but we don't yet know the mental condition of Salfrod, due to the violent blow to the head that he took. I would say the aim of his attacker was not just to render him unconscious, but to kill him."

"I'm afraid, Captain, that you may not get as much out of our stowaway as you might hope," came the disappointing news from Dr. Karushkin. "His injuries, while not rendering him brain dead, have seriously hampered his memory and reasoning ability. He will probably respond to only the basic of questions and any more than that will either confuse him or greatly upset him. In either case, you will not receive any satisfactory answers unless you keep your questions very simple. I would suggest you attempt to gain his trust as you would a small child. For indeed that is what you are dealing with."

Captain Keanyn Mathews looked dejectedly at the three others he had brought with him, and Mac was the only one who volunteered any comment. In fact, there was an eagerness in her bright green eyes as she said, "I think I can handle that, Captain! After all, I had to win the trust of my hard-headed younger brother and that was no small task. Commander Loche has some experience in that, but he is quite a bit older than Edward, and I think this will need the feminine touch."

"I think that is probably a good way to start, Commander," Captain Mathews replied. "I don't have much experience with young children being an only child. But, child-like or not, we must still get some definitive answers from him. How do you propose to do that, Ms. Stinson?"

He turned and looked into her eyes, which appeared full of confidence, and she said, "The good doctor mentioned winning Salfrod's trust, and I know how far commendation and persuasion can get you with a child who is nervous and eager to please. So, if you'll follow my lead, I think we can get at least some satisfactory answers."

They entered sick bay and were directed to a small enclosure to the left of the main exam room. Propped up part way in his bed lay the stowaway, with bandages wrapped around the top of his head and down around his forehead. His facial features were clear, and the third nostril was very apparent. He was looking around with the bewilderment of a young child of about six or seven years old, and as he caught sight of his guests, his look changed to that of apprehension and a little fear.

Mac took a slow step or two forward, smiling, and said in a quiet, reassuring voice, "Hello, my name is Mac, and we are all very glad to see that you are feeling better. Dr Karushkin tells us your name is Salfrod. Is that right?" She tilted her head slightly, in what she hoped was a gesture that said "I'm your friend, you can talk to me."

It apparently worked as Salfrod relaxed a bit and nodded his head in confirmation of his name.

Mac continued, "Since we didn't know that you were on this ship, we didn't have the opportunity to welcome you aboard. And since the first time we saw you was after you had been injured, we have been hoping that we would be able to get to know you." She was trying to make him feel that he was safe among friends with no fear of having done anything wrong.

She looked over at Dr. Karushkin, who smiled and gave her a nod of approval, encouraging her to continue along this line of questioning.

"I hope you don't mind if I ask you a few questions just so we can get to know you better? If you're not able to answer, don't worry, we know your injury has affected your memory a bit. So, it's not your fault."

Salfrod winced at the mention of his injury's effect on his memory, but he straightened up and spoke for the first time. "I like Dr. Karushkin. He's been nice to me and has made me feel better. I think I like you too, lady." He stopped abruptly as he looked embarrassed and pulled the covers slightly up over his head.

Mac chuckled as she gazed back at Salfrod with sympathy. Whatever conspiratorial or violent deed had brought the stowaway on the ship in the first place was currently replaced with an innocent and genuinely fearful demeanor. He was no longer a threat to them, but they hoped he could still provide some answers.

"Salfrod, do you remember how you got on this ship?" She tried to make it easier for him with a little coaxing. "I mean, did someone put you on the ship or were you transferred from another ship?'

Salfrod got a little more excited when she mentioned being transferred and said, "I think that was it. I mean that transferred thing. I think I was on another ship before I got on this one."

They all looked at each other with the thought that "maybe we're getting somewhere now."

Grannison raised a finger to get Mac's attention and said, "Could I try a question?"

"Certainly" was her reply.

He spoke with a surprisingly higher pitch to his usually deep voice, saying "Do you remember if the other ship had a Masking Transfer Unit? I mean something that would keep your transfer secret from this ship? I remember I used to play hide-and-seek like that when I was a kid. It was fun."

"I don't remember if we had one of those masking

things, and I can't remember playing any games, but I do remember somebody saying that the ambassador said we were allowed to do it."

A slight gasp came from Mac and the others. Salfrod noticed the reactions and said, "Ah! Do you know the ambassador?"

Robert Porter was the one who replied by saying "We know several ambassadors, and one of them is on this ship. His name is Yahnsoof Callurran and he happens to be from the planet your ship last left from." Robert knew that a direct statement used at the right time can catch a person off guard, causing them to slip up in their speech and either give something away or innocently divulge information that was critical.

Salfrod did not seem to be bothered by the statement as noted by his open reply. "I can't remember what planet I was on before I came here, and I don't know the ambassador's name. They just kept calling him the ambassador."

Robert and the others knew he was not trying to be evasive because his injuries had affected his memory. He simply was unaware that he was under any kind of suspicion or that he needed to feel guilty about anything.

Dr. Karushkin noticed that Salfrod was showing signs of fatigue and suggested that they wrap up the questions for the time being. Keanyn politely asked if they could try one more question and the doctor acquiesced.

The captain asked, "Salfrod, do you remember why you were coming to this ship in the first place?"

The patient looked upward as if to concentrate and, after about a ten-second pause, said, "I think it had something to do with changing something on this ship." He smiled and looked at them as if he was seeking their approval and yawned.

"You must have been coming to help us fix something, but since we couldn't find any paperwork on you when we found you, the person who hurt you must have taken it. That person will be in a lot of trouble when we find him!" Mac said this to him so that he wouldn't feel like he was in any trouble and that he didn't need to be afraid for himself.

Following this, Salfrod fell immediately asleep with a look on his face of complete peace and contentment.

Dr. Karushkin escorted the foursome out of sick bay and noted, "I thought that you handled that interrogation in the proper manner given the patient's condition, but his answers give me grave concerns about his mission and the highly possible involvement of Ambassador Callurran."

Captain Mathews looked at the doctor with determination in his eyes as he said, "I'm sure we share those same concerns, Doctor. I know I do, and we will make certain we get to the bottom of this!"

When they returned to the captain's quarters for further consultation, Grannison Loche spoke first.

"Captain, I think I can find something out from the shuttle bay's records that might give us some information concerning Salfrod's arrival on the mall starship. I've had a lot of experience flying shuttles and other small craft and have learned the inner workings of a lot of their systems, including transporting, masking and the like. There's a good chance I can find out when the exact transfer was made, from what distance it was done, how many were on that ship, and, more importantly, who was on the shuttle waiting for him on this ship."

Keanyn's answer to that was "Why didn't you suggest all of this earlier?"

"Because it will take three or four days to figure it out, and I thought we might get some quick answers from our interview with Salfrod. But when I saw how limited his information was going to be due to his injuries, I realized I would have to try my plan," came the answer from Grannison.

Robert was looking thoughtful as he turned to Keanyn and said, "I would like to join Commander Loche in his investigative endeavor to see if he can find any answers to other questions I have concerning Mr. Salfrod's activities. If you don't mind, Captain?

"I think that is a great idea, Mr. Porter," Keanyn said and then turned to look at Mac, saying "Have you got any thoughts you would like to pursue?"

Mac turned to the captain and said, "I would like to find out what else our uninvited guest was doing on Saffo V during the three days he spent there before coming here. It seems likely to me that he could have made additional arrangements and met with other individuals that may interest us. I have some contacts in the scientific community there and one or two of them keep their eyes and ears open for unusual activity that could affect our mission."

Grannison asked, with a hint of surprise in his voice, "How did you come to have informants on a planet that has been pretty well dead set against this project from the beginning?"

Mac replied, "I've been having some conversations with our head of security and he's been kind enough to school me in a few of the techniques in the information-gathering field. He wanted to know if I had any contacts on Saffo V that I could trust. He felt that certain information from the scientific field might prove to be invaluable to us in our investigation."

As she said this, she watched Keanyn out of the corner of her eye and noted a slight frown form on his face at the mention of her "private" tutoring from the head of security. She thought to herself, *I wonder if that's a sign of jealousy for me or the information Robert shared with me.* She continued her answer to Grannison. "As to the unlikely scenario of someone on Saffo V willing to help the earth in our mission, the two fellow scientists I contacted graduated with me and come from planets sympathetic to our goal and were assigned to Ambassador Callurran's planet to try and mend the rift that exists between them and us."

"I see," said Grannison, "and while they were at it, they might also take note of any other information that might come their way?"

"Something like that" was Robert Porter's answer. He continued, "In any case, I felt that the information they could give might be too technical for me to understand, and knowing our science officer's brilliant intellect, I knew she'd be the perfect agent for the task."

Keanyn motioned for Porter and Loche to join him in an adjoining room. Once inside, he spoke with some fervor, saying "It sounds like you recruited her as a spy, not just asked her for a favor. I mean agent! Really, Mr. Porter, she is primarily our science officer, or has she turned in her notice and joined your employ?"

Robert and Grannison both looked at the captain with open-mouth stares, wondering at his uncharacteristic outburst.

Captain Keanyn Mathews had surprised himself with his spirited comment. He noted the expressions on the two men's faces, lightly shook his head, and looked upon them with determination and said, "I won't apologize for my outburst, gentlemen. I feel the need to emphasize that we can't go around recruiting people for a mission without going through proper channels. Having said that, I am glad that we have another line of inquiry into this investigation and that the Lieutenant Commander can use her scientific skills in this regard." He gave the two of them a stern look but softened his visage as he calmly put a hand on each of their shoulders, saying "I know that whatever you do is for the safety and well-being of this ship, its mission, and its crew. But as captain, I must be informed of your ideas and how they will affect my crew."

"What I did was impetuous and inconsiderate of your authority, sir," said Robert humbly. "I will be more careful in the future."

"Thank you, Commander," said Keanyn. "I am anxious to see how Head Science Officer Stinson does as a secret operative." He smiled conspiratorially at the other two who returned the smile as they saluted him.

With that tense moment resolved, they returned to the conference room. Shortly after that, Stenn and ND arrived, with Cheng coming in a few minutes later. As everyone got seated, Keanyn suggested that the new arrivals fill them in on whatever they had discovered.

Cheng started things off. "The closest I could get to the exact time of Salfrod's arrival is some two and a half hours before his discovery. The masking of his transfer makes it difficult to get it any closer and it was only by tweaking some settings that we can get it that close." She looked frustrated to have to give such a less-than-satisfactory report, but she revived when being told of Grannison's plan to uncover some answers and volunteered to help him.

This was agreed upon, and Keanyn asked her, "Did you find out about anyone being near the shuttle about that time?"

"Yes," she said. "There wasn't much activity since the shuttle bay was not in use. But that's good since any prolonged activity would be suspicious and easy to spot, and we came on two incidents."

Robert Porter chimed in, "Were either of them significant to our situation?"

"One seemed more so than the other" was Cheng's reply. She continued, "A group of Sharlees came very near the shuttle and stopped relatively close to it. They seemed to be horsing around—as is their custom—but when they left, I could have sworn that there was one less in their group. I didn't notice any of them leave the group as we watched, but there was a lot of activity among them as they were having their fun."

The rest of the group had looks ranging from suspicion to amusement. The amusement was due to the frivolous nature of Sharlees, and this just seemed like more of that. The suspicion was felt by the three you would have expected: Robert, Stenn and ND. In fact, Stenn was the next to speak and his tone showed no amusement whatsoever.

"I hope you ran that vid through many more times in different speeds and resolutions to try and get a better grasp on just what happened!"

Cheng was a bit perturbed by his tone and question but managed to keep her voice calm, if not a little stern. "Why yes, Stenn. We did spend a lot of time studying that vid and ran it through several speeds as well as bumping up its clarity as much as we could and still keep it discernible."

"And what were your conclusions following your rigorous and commendable efforts, Lieutenant Cheng?" said the captain, attempting to ease the tension that had developed in the room.

Cheng breathed a short sigh and, with a genuine smile on her face, said, "We noticed a particular fuzziness in the quality of the video for a brief minute. When there was a lot of frantic activity within the group. I can't be certain what the activity was because of the fuzziness. While it may have been any number of things, it could have been the motion of someone leaving the group, and it was after this that the group of Sharlees seemed to be just a bit smaller."

Mac was looking at Cheng with an expression of bewilderment and said, "With no disrespect to your powers of observation, Cheng, if someone did leave the group, wouldn't you have seen them going in a different direction, or at least standing apart from the group as they left the area? I mean, that's a fairly open space around the shuttles with not many places to hide."

"I am just as perplexed as you are, Mac, and, undoubtedly, all the rest of you. It's as if anyone who may have left the group vanished into thin air," remarked Cheng incredulously.

"Well," said ND, "the best we can do, under the circumstances, is to file this away and keep a watchful eye on the Sharlee contingent here on the ship. I know that seems a bit surprising given their nature. Even I would normally consider the Sharlees the last people to suspect of any malicious subterfuge."

Captain Mathews looked toward his second-in-command and noticed that Grannison was staring straight ahead with a look of deep concentration. Keanyn knew that Grannison Loche had a very analytical mind and so he said to him, "Commander Loche, I can hear the wheels in your brain moving from here. What have you got on your mind?"

"No great revelation I assure you, Captain. I was just

thinking that when I go to help Cheng with the masking that took place on that shuttle, I could also look into this incident and see if there isn't some way a person could vanish into thin air."

"I know you like a challenge, but this may be one too tough to crack," said the captain. "Nevertheless, I would not deny you the chance to try. With that said," he added, "I'd like to ask Lieutenant Commander Porter if he wouldn't mind being asked to team with Stenn in investigating the Sharlee incident, as we'll call it. I think two sharp minds will be needed for that." He received a nod of approval from Robert and turned back to Cheng, saying "You mentioned a second incident of note on the vids, Lieutenant."

"Yes, sir, it was a group of mechanics who arrived at the shuttle and appeared to do work on it," she remarked. "While I usually am informed of those things, I checked and they did have a proper work order. Still, oversights like that don't sit well with me."

"Did you double-check that work order's authorization?" asked Keanyn.

"Yes, sir!" Exclaimed Cheng. "What I found was the second copy of the work order, that normally comes to me, stuffed into the file with a note to pass it onto me. It had, apparently, gotten shoved into the file by accident before it could get to me."

"Were you okay with that, Lieutenant Wong?" the captain posed.

She answered with a slight pause. "At first, sir. But with the addition of what we have considered here, I am not so sure now."

Robert Porter broke into the discussion, saying "If you will excuse me, Captain, there are several red flags going off in my head. It is my opinion that Lieutenant Wong should revisit those two vids, with the help of Commander Loche, and see what else may be gleaned from them."

"I agree," said the captain.

That seemed to satisfy everyone and that left only one more report.

Keanyn had decided that whatever Stenn and his mother had to report, it might be better to have them give that to him in private as he had noticed the reluctance they had displayed when he had told everyone that they, along with Cheng, would give their reports to the group. He knew that they often unearthed very delicate information that they only shared with Robert Porter and his assistant, Ross Carter, until it was felt that more people needed to know. He told the rest of the group that because of duties he needed to see to, time did not permit them to hear the report of ND and her son at that time. He noticed the looks of relief on the faces of the two undercover investigators and added to the rest, "Don't worry, I'll make sure you're all briefed on their findings." That seemed to satisfy everyone, and they all went to their separate assignments.

Chapter 13

The A Deck

When the meeting of the Stowaway Investigative Team adjourned, ND whispered to Keanyn that if he followed her and her son back to her quarters, they would give their report to him there. Keanyn agreed but let them know that he really did have to go to the bridge to make sure that all of the bridge crew had everything in hand. He said, "If you're the captain of a starship and you haven't been on the bridge for several hours, the crew will either think you don't care or that, since everything has been running smoothly without you, you're not needed, and that would be a terrible blow to their confidence in the person they are supposed to look to for leadership."

"I can certainly understand that, Captain" was ND's reply. She added, "When would you like to receive our report?"

Keanyn looked thoughtful and said, "I need to be on the bridge for at least four hours. Then, if there are no emergencies, I should be able to come to your quarters. We only have about three and a half days to conclude our investigation before our first visitors arrive, and all the reports need to be analyzed in order to accomplish that, as you well know." Keanyn's concern was matched by both Stenn and his mother.

"We will most certainly need all of this vital information before we can move significantly forward," Stenn stated.

It was agreed that the three of them would get together in five hours in ND's quarters, and that is where they found themselves at that precise time.

Keanyn sat down at the table in the sitting room of ND's quarters and took a drink from the fluted wine glass that sat there. A bottle sat in the middle of the table with three filled glasses at each chair. When Keanyn had swallowed, he looked at ND with a smile of approval, saying "That's some of the best Mardovian champagne I've ever tasted. My compliments." With that, he tilted his glass in a salute to his hostess.

ND nodded her appreciation, accompanied by her enigmatic smile. "Being in the deep-cover investigative field does have some perks, Captain. I or my son frequently receive gifts, as it were, for our services by either appreciative clients or, sometimes, ones who would rather we not report our findings for their—shall we say—protection? That particular bottle of 2204 Mardovian is part of a case of six from a client who just begged us to take it. It seems that what we had uncovered made him fear for his life, and since what we had learned was not technically illegal, we were willing to accede to his wishes of not revealing it."

Stenn added, "Don't think we are susceptible to bribery,

Captain. Our acceptance of gifts is either from genuine appreciation by our clients or, as in the case of the champagne, extra payment for the safety of our client. If definite criminal activity is not involved or the statute of limitations has expired, but harm to our client may still come from certain other parties, we do accept such gifts in order to assure them of our silence."

"I appreciate your sharing of this gift with me," Keanyn stated sincerely. "I'm certainly glad we have the benefit of your services on this mission, and I'm glad that your good friend Lieutenant Porter was able to convince you of our need to have you with us."

ND again nodded her head in appreciative agreement of the captain's sincere comment. "It didn't take much convincing for two reasons. The first is that we have been very close to Robert for nearly a decade, and we feel that we have been entrusted to train him in ways that his father and his schooling could not hope to. So that if he was going into space on a mission of such singular importance, we would need to be near him. Secondly, our investigations had helped him come to the conclusion of the very real possibility of sabotage, so we felt an obligation to be here to help him thwart such a possibility."

Keanyn responded with a smile and said, "Your loyal friendship to Robert is also proving to be a boon to this mission and the crew as well, and I thank you. Now it's time to include your latest findings into the further investigation of the stowaway and whatever link he may have to sabotage. Stenn, fill me in."

"As you know, Captain, I and Mac had already done some preliminary snooping. It seems that Salfrod's ship had dangerously diminished supplies of cagnogite, the catalyst used to activate the fuel that propelled the thrusters on Salfrod's ship, which I found out is called the *Vecton*, which is a transliteration of the Cherillian word for the *Hawk*.

"As you may know, cagnogite is only found on a handful of planets, and one of them is Saffo V. That could explain why the *Hawk* landed there. But here's the really interesting point."

Stenn paused to make sure that he had Keanyn's full attention. "Mac learned that Salfrod had informed the ambassador of the situation during his last communication and the ambassador said that, by all means, he was to make certain that the *Hawk* was moved to the ambassador's launch pad in order to inject the cagnogite into the thruster engines. Mac's scientist/informant was called on to supervise the operation."

Keanyn interrupted, "Why would they need the supervision of a scientist for a procedure more suited to a simple mechanic or maybe an engineer?"

Stenn looked over at his mother and motioned for her to give a closer ear to what he was about to say. "This is some information I haven't, as yet, shared with my mother. It seems that when anyone receives a shipment of thruster fuel for a fleet of ships or when anyone refuels at another planet, the cagnogite is already mixed with the rest of the fuel's ingredients. The process of mixing the two together requires a very complicated chemical procedure that must be supervised by a chemical engineer. An improper mixture of cagnogite with the main fuel will cause a horrific explosion as will the mixing of the two too rapidly. Mac's informant happens to have a degree in chemical engineering and was able to supply the information to her."

"Thank you for that enlightening piece of information, son," said ND "Do you have any more information?"

"Indeed I do," Stenn said. "I was able to discover most of Salfrod's companions on the *Hawk,* and there are two of particular note. One is an ex-convict from Cherula, Salfrod's home planet, named Kelrad Galdalene."

Once again, Keanyn interrupted. "I've heard that name. My father told me that he was one of the resistance fighters whose troop gave him fits just after the Legion's arrival. It seems he and several other Cherillians, along with a few stragglers and discontents from other planets, would swoop in and make lightning-quick raids on supply ships and the early Earth trainees at the new Legion military facilities."

"Yes," said Stenn, "one and the same. But here's the even more interesting thing about what I found. The captain of the ship they used was a nephew of Ambassador Callurran named Ansmed and the name of the small star cruiser they flew was the *Vecton* or the *Hawk*!"

Keanyn looked like someone had just thrown a bucket of cold water on him. He gasped when he said, "Good grief! The same ship that blasted off from Saffo V with our buddy, Salfrod?"

"Yes, but a decommissioned Legion ship that was taken out of mothballs and completely retooled and modified with cutting-edge masking capabilities by the aforementioned Ansmed. He used the connections he had made as the ambassador's nephew to obtain his old star cruiser and get her tricked out," answered Stenn as he calmly sat his empty glass of champagne on the table.

Keanyn was still a bit confused. "Wouldn't Ansmed have been considered a criminal by the Legion and especially by Saffo V for his resistance activity?"

Stenn replied, "Most definitely! But remember that was nearly thirty years ago, and while he was in the incarceration colony on Practaurus in the Perseus arm, he was a model prisoner and was released seven years ago. When he learned that the *Cosmic Mall* was nearing completion and his uncle's involvement with it, he feigned interest in it and got back in the good graces of his uncle. Or he learned of his uncle's duplicity and formed a conspiracy with him. Which of those is true, I have not discovered. With that, my report is complete." As he finished his disclosure, Stenn poured himself a second glass of the Mardovian, and sat back in his chair with a satisfied look.

His mother sat forward in her chair and gently moved a lock of her black and golden hair away from her left eye in a motion akin to a mild summer breeze. She said, "I now see that my conversation with the ambassador was even more interesting than I thought."

"Ah, yes," said Keanyn, "I have yet to hear from you, Madam ND. What savory gems have you to add to this complex investigation?"

ND also poured another glass of the Mardovian, held it up to the light, swirled it around once or twice, and gently sniffed its bouquet before she took a drink. This is, of course, the standard practice of any wine connoisseur, but she made it look like the graceful movement of a ballet dancer. She then said, "The ambassador and I had a lovely afternoon tea, rounded out by a humorous and revealing conversation. It seems that Yhansoof—forgive me, but it was a casual conversation in informal surroundings, and the ambassador and I have an amiable relationship, so we are perfectly comfortable using our first names."

She was immediately prevented from continuing by Keanyn, who said, "He calls you by your first name? With the exception of your son here, none of the rest of us know what your first name is. So does he just call you "N" or what?"

There was a subtle smile on ND's face as she answered.

"My dear Captain Mathews. For the sole purpose of our informal conversations, he calls me Madeline. He says he feels that the name is elegant and sophisticated and fits my personality and demeanor. Therefore, I allow him to call me by that name, though it is not correct. It is also agreeable to me because I am not unfond of the name." She took another sip of her champagne looking over its rim as she focused her blue eyes on the captain.

Keanyn found it difficult to maintain his composure under the stare of such a beautiful and graceful woman. After about five seconds of silence, he answered her.

"Madeline certainly is a name that would fit you, but I have derailed this conversation from its initial purpose, and I apologize. Please, ND, continue with your report."

"Thank you, Captain. As we talked, I inconspicuously directed the conversation toward his home planet on the basis that I would like to visit his home sometime in the future. He then described his domicile with such a fondness that I asked if he was feeling a little homesick. He replied that having to be away so often in his capacity as an ambassador naturally ignites a longing for his home from time to time. He then added that the positive result of his absence from his cherished home was that, when he did return there, he was able to renew his love for it all over again."

She paused, then sighed and brought her gaze back to the other two occupants in the room. "I'm sorry, gentlemen, but I'm trying to keep my fondness for the ambassador from influencing this investigation. You need not worry that I am unable to accomplish that, but I do need to stop and take stalk of the situation from time to time. Moving forward, we now come to the part of our conversation that was, particularly, interesting.

"While describing his house and its grounds, Yhansoof

began discussing his launching port and seemed very proud of its state-of-the-art capabilities. I encouraged him to speak further about it and he obliged by saying that a ship designed and flown by his nephew had recently launched from his port when he had to land on Saffo V because of thruster fuel problems. He said that his launch port was one of only two on the planet that could mix and install the highly volatile fuel in a ship's thruster engines. He then abruptly ended the conversation with the not-so-convincing excuse that he was boring me with all of these silly details, and when I assured him he was not boring me in any way, he just waved it off and changed the subject."

"That's highly interesting," said Stenn. "It seems that the good ambassador may have revealed more by what he didn't say than by what he did."

"My thoughts exactly, Stenn," remarked Keanyn, who then turned to ND, saying "Was there any more of interest you can add?"

"Just one more thing," noted ND. "As we were saying our goodbyes, Ambassador Callurran gently touched my shoulder and with an embarrassed grin, asked if I would not repeat his statements about his launch pad as it may sound as if he was bragging, and that would not aid his ambassadorial responsibilities if people thought that he was overly proud of his possessions. It seemed to me that he was trying to save face and make sure that he wouldn't be perceived as a risk by others."

Keanyn responded, "What did you say in return to him?"

ND had a look as if she were still ruminating on her comment to the ambassador. "I told him he should have nothing to worry about since it had just been a casual conversation between friends, and that I wasn't in the habit of relating our conversations to other people."

"Well," said Stenn, "as incriminating as all of that sounds, we still can't be certain if Ambassador Callurran is involved in any plot to thwart the mission of this starship."

"That's true," stated Keanyn. "But he sure isn't doing himself any favors. He seems to be rising in my estimation of his guilt. How about you two?"

ND answered first. "While I agree that his participation in a possible sabotage plot is becoming more certain, I can't discount his genuine and open attitude during our conversations. It is difficult for me to see him as such a deceiver and manipulator."

Stenn chimed in with a contradictory comment. "Mother, you are the last person I would imagine to be taken in by a smooth-talking con artist, but your conversations with Callurran may have affected your naturally suspicious attitude."

"I appreciate your concern, son, but I promise you, my suspicions concerning the ambassador have not been affected. I am still quite ready to accept the strong possibility of his involvement in a conspiracy. Add to that my assurance to you that I am still quite capable of detecting the duplicity of the smooth-talking con man. That is why I find it difficult to reconcile the strong circumstantial evidence of his guilt with the genuineness of his casual conversations with me. I have listened for the evidence of his conning me in his voice and I can find none." It was clear in her tone of voice that she was perplexed by this dilemma, but ND was not about to give in to sentimentality. She added, "Also, we need to consider that I have not given the ambassador any reason to feel that I suspect him of anything, so there would be no reason for him trying to deceive me."

Keanyn jumped back into the conversation by saying "I

think it is safe to say that Ambassador Callurran is still high on our list of suspects while maintaining that the evidence does not make that a certainty. Would that be a reasonable assessment?"

Both ND and her son agreed and decided to put their latest investigative results before the rest of the team and get their views.

By the end of the day, the entire team had been informed of the findings of ND and Stenn, and agreed with Keanyn's assessment of them. Grannison added an extra tidbit he had discovered while helping Cheng with the shuttle vids.

"We discovered that when Salfrod made the transfer from the *Hawk* to here, he was completely alone on that ship. Where the rest of the crew had gotten to, we could not discover, though, it was a certainty that they had departed Saffo V on board the *Hawk*."

Captain Keanyn Mathews scratched his head in bewilderment as he remarked, "This case gets more perplexing the more we uncover. Have you been able to come up with any indication of who it might have been that greeted our stowaway with a blow to his head?"

"Nothing conclusive," said Grannison. "But it appears that whoever was waiting for him engaged him in conversation for several minutes before striking him. We were able to extract some feedback from the voice analyzers on board. Mind you, we weren't able to extract any actual words, but we were able to ascertain that the voice other than Salfrod's was female and that as the conversation continued, she became increasingly upset."

"That could have precipitated the physical violence," stated Keanyn. "Keep digging, Grann, but we'll need you on the bridge in two hours for our exit from MLS and our docking at the orbital station for our first planetary visit."

"Aye aye, Captain." It is to be noted that, while the reply was respectful, there was a hint of humor to it, and it wasn't lost on the captain who, with a twinkle in his eye and a smile on his lips, answered, "Very good, Commander."

The most unusual feature of the Starship *Cosmic Mall* was what has been previously called the circular plate. It was a circular, metal-like structure of a circumference approximately one-third that of the fuselage. Its most frequent position resembled that of a disc underneath the horizontal shaft that led from the vertical lift to the ship's fuselage and appeared to sit right against it. This disc could be deployed by moving it forward until it sat completely in front of the ship as an extended floor space. In emergency situations, this disc could be raised to a vertical position with its underside facing out. This side of the disc was made of the aforementioned 'Strell' and could then be used as the battering ram if the situation ever presented itself. There was a central supportive beam that ran up the middle of the disc whose outer side was slightly convex. It was, also, from this beam that an extra and more powerful defensive shielding could be deployed.

This circular plate stood out as the very front of the ship, but not so much so that it appeared to be disproportionate to the rest of the structure. This structure had one more feature that was highly unique. To explain that, we must look into the not-too-distant history of the Galactic Legion nearly eight decades previously.

Seventy-eight years earlier, the Legion had established an engineering colony on the planet of Balnyx, a rather inhospitable planet in the Keplar twenty system. With the atmosphere not conducive to most sentient life forms, and not possessing any minerals worth mining, it was thought to be an excellent location for undisturbed engineering research and development.

The most innovative results of the research coming from the Balnyx colony was purely accidental.

After several years, the majority of the engineers working in the colony's structures were getting tired of the limited views afforded them from those structures. They could, of course, go outside if properly protected, but this was extremely limiting. They decided to see if they could come up with a way to enjoy unobstructed views of their planetary surroundings as well as the starry skies around them. It took them twelve years to develop a system that could accomplish that, and it was only made available for the Legion's use after rigorous testing that was completed only fourteen years previously.

It was decided, by the Legion, to implement the use of this discovery for the first time on the Starship *Cosmic Mall*, and the disc was the perfect place for it. That meant that it would have to be installed quickly because the mall ship was entering the final phase of construction.

The unique development made by the engineers on Balnyx was the creation of walls made of pure atmosphere. No visible signs of support were evident. These walls of atmosphere were as safe as any of the others on the ship. They could give a person a completely unobstructed 360-degree view. In its horizontal position at the bow of the ship, the disc, within its atmospheric protection, would serve as the ultimate viewing platform and entertainment venue for visitors to the galaxy's most singular attraction.

The housing for the "walls" were in the four-and-a-half-foot-deep hollow interior of the plate secured by doors that opened and closed by a crew member of the ship located in the "A" deck control room. The atmospheric walls could then be deployed with their attachment to the inner central beam to effectively make them one "solid" wall.

Therefore, the rather drab moniker of "The Circular Disc" became known as "The A deck."

Stenn had been working feverishly to narrow down the planned location of the suspected sabotage and had gotten it down to two. The mall itself or the A deck.

He and Ross Carter doubled the security to be used for the visiting dignitaries from their first stop on Drathon III in the Eridean system. In connection with the A deck, Stenn, along with Robert Porter, had tightened up the security involving the control room that housed the computers and other mechanisms for the operation of the "Atmospheric" deck. They had recoded the locking mechanisms on the entry and exit portal. Then, they reduced the personnel allowed in that room to three (in addition to the captain, Robert Porter, Stenn, and Chief Engineer Davis). In addition, they had upgraded the fail-safe function to insure against accidental shutdown of the system.

While the actual mechanics for the raising and lowering of the A deck were housed in the lower or bottom side of the plate, along with a housing on the top of the central beam, to which the plate was attached, the actual controls were in the A deck control room, a small twelve-by-sixteen-foot room in the bottom floor of the vertical lift.

When the deck had been cleared of life forms, the walls were retracted into the storage area, and the A deck was moved back to its position under the horizontal shaft.

These added precautions had been finally set in place mere hours before the mall starship docked at the space port for Drathon III.

The commander of the scout ship, *Crockett*, Captain Zach Demopolis, communicated to Captain Keanyn Mathews: "The inhabitants of Legion Planet Drathon Three are ready to accept your invitation to board the Starship *Cosmic Mall,* Captain. And, might I say, a more eager and childishly pleasant group you may never meet. I think the VIP entourage may be the most excited of the entire population of the planet."

"It sounds as if you and your crew did your job of hyping us up very well," came the reply of Captain Mathews. He continued, "I just hope you didn't do it too well and we can live up to all the hype. Ambassador Callurran is especially anxious to meet his old friend Chairman Hillian, head of the Ruling Council."

Zach replied, "The chairman is also keenly desirous of seeing the ambassador again. You may also wish to focus your attentions on Craidek Marn, the secretary of commerce, and Ms. Lulianna Wasnova, the most renowned operatic diva on Drathon Three. Her voice is almost as powerful as a stun torpedo. She is, perhaps, the most popular and influential person on the planet."

"I will be certain to direct my considerable charm in her direction, Zach" was the comment of the captain of the mall starship.

Zach said, "Well, there goes all the hard work I put into setting this planet up for our visit."

"Very funny," said Keanyn and the two old friends signed off.

It was now time for another historic first in the history-setting mission of Earth's contribution to the Galactic Legion. Most of the officers and crew of the starship were joyously looking forward to this significant event. A few were nervous and anxious because of the duties and responsibilities they had. Yet another group were extremely apprehensive in light of the potential disaster that might occur.

Some of those included among the nervous were those who were standing at the main entrance to the mall that led into a sizeable vestibule that served as a buffer between the cavernous shuttle bay and the eye-popping glow of the shopping mall. The grand entrance to the mall that greeted visitors was a cornucopia of colors and lights. It could be an overload to the senses after the military-like bleakness of the shuttle bay.

The decision to keep the mall starship docked in a planet's space port instead of landing on the planet itself was twofold. First, by remaining off planet, it made the transporting of the planet's residents much easier as they could board the shuttles from various locations on the surface more convenient to them, and second, the mall ship was so large that special arrangements would have to be made to accommodate it on the planet's surface if at all.

The small welcoming committee, as it were, consisted of the mall's owner Clarice Pickle, her mall manager, Saffaw, Assistant Security Chief Ross Carter. Also present were Stella Steel and Larindoo kwark, the main botanists in charge of the plant and floral arrangements that made up a large part of the mall's stunning beauty. In addition were the managers of each of the twelve huge anchor stores.

These seventeen individuals stood in a half circle, two deep, in front of a slightly raised speaker's podium, behind which stood Mrs. Pickle. As the eighteen-member VIP contingent from Drathon III emerged from the exit to the vestibule with Cheng Wong, the commander of the shuttle deck, serving as their guide, Clarice spread her arms in a grand welcoming gesture and said, "It is my great honor to welcome our most distinguished visitors from Drathon Three and to wish Chairman Hillian and the rest of you who represent the finest minds and talents in all of the Eridean system the warmest of greetings. We are especially pleased to be graced by the presence of Ms. Lulianna Wasnova, whose incredible talent precedes her and from whom we hope to enjoy even the smallest snippet of an aria."

This speech was given by Clarice in the native tongue of Drathon III and had been a source of nervous anxiety for her over the last ten days in which she had studied feverishly to learn it phonetically.

The visiting dignitaries smiled and bowed their heads slightly in recognition and acceptance of the flowery greeting, with Chairman Hillian adding the comment, "It is we who are honored to be the initial invitees to this most exceptional endeavor, 'the Starship *Cosmic Mall*.' And may I add that it is a most satisfactory honor to be addressed by you in our native language. We thank you and can't wait for our tours to commence. I understand that we will be divided into three groups of six each and be given tours of three different areas of the mall?"

Ross Carter responded to this question. "Yes, that is true. The mall is so large and there are many events you will be attending in the coming days that we felt this was the most practical way to allow your delegation to see the entire facility."

"We Drathonites highly esteem practicality and, therefore, find your decision to divide our group up as a most acceptable one," came the amiable response of Craidek Marn, Drathon III's secretary of commerce.

After the three groups were selected and each of them led, respectively, by Clarice, Saffaw, and Ross, the tours began in earnest.

In the next four and a half hours, the three groups were introduced to a vast array of shopping and entertainment experiences. From the small kiosks selling a variety of products, like Vaneese pottery that featured multiple chambers with their own pouring spouts, to the exotic but very small plants and flowers of the totally forested world of Silva.

They also had the particular experience of enjoying the culinary delights from any number of Legion planets.

Then there were the variety of products sold within each of the twelve anchor stores. The glass-like power tools from Dulgannia which were more durable than any ever made on Earth and really caught the eyes of many in the group on that tour.

The extravaganza of entertainment dazzled the visitors as well and the high-wire and trapeze acts, bringing many an exclamation of awe and wonder from the Drathonite dignitaries.

Throughout all of these events, there was not even a hint of any disturbance or unwanted trouble. Whatever minor hitches occurred were easily remedied.

The VIP tours of the mall having come off without a hitch, Ross Carter breathed a tentative sigh of relief. He reminded himself that this was only the beginning of the first visit and that the huge reception on the A deck was coming up tomorrow night. Having been informed by his boss, Robert Porter, that the A deck was the other primary location for the possible sabotage, Ross knew that his need to be especially watchful would continue throughout their stay at Drathon III.

"Well, I couldn't be more overjoyed at the success of the

tours and the obviously impressed reaction of our visitors," came the subdued but excited voice at his shoulder of Clarice Pickle. "I congratulate you and your associates on a job well done," she continued. "If I hadn't known they were there, I never would have guessed that we were being shadowed by your expert team of protectors."

"Thank you, Mrs. Pickle, but as they say, that's why they pay us the big bucks," came the reply of the assistant chief of security. He added a cautionary comment. "While the tour of the mall was certainly a major highlight of their visit, it is only the first of several opportunities for trouble in the nine more days left on this initial port-of-call. We can't let our guard down for a minute."

"So Stenn and his mother keep telling me," replied Clarice. "In any case, I am perfectly content to leave those details to you and Mr. Porter. At least my beautiful mall has been spared any sabotage for now, and I can concentrate more fully on seeing that this initial visit becomes the fabulous showcase for this mall that I have planned on making it."

Saffaw, who had been within earshot of the conversation, chimed in, "I'm certain Mrs. Pickle meant that the planning of the ten-day extravaganza for this awesome retail edifice was a joint effort between myself and her. It would, of course, take the combined effort of great visionary minds like ours to create and implement the festivities that are about to unfold before your eyes."

"'A great visionary mind'?" said Clarice incredulously. "You, Saffaw, are suffering from delusions of grandeur. You may have contributed a point or two, but make no mistake, the upcoming festivities have little to do with any input you may have made. I will give you credit that you will be able to manage the various events. After all, that is why I hired you. But you do not have a creative nor visionary bone in your alien body!"

Saffaw feigned a hurtful expression but came back with the retort "You may be my employer, Mrs. Pickle, but the statement that you alone are responsible for the events to take place during the next nine days is simply ludicrous. I'll grant that you might have envisioned some of the proceedings, but I and others contributed ideas as well. What about Louise Munoz whom Captain Paxton of the *Gator* so generously lent to us and her wonderful high-wire and trapeze acts? Her background in the circus makes her the perfect person to head up your entertainment committee."

Clarice was by no means shaken from her stance by Saffaw's comment and said, "The ability to know how to use individuals in incorporating one's plans is the hallmark of any great visionary. Therefore, my use of such ones as Lieutenant Munoz is perfectly within the scope of my creative mind." As she said this, she stood up tall, thrusting her chin out in a very commanding and definitive posture.

Ross Carter had been standing quietly by as the two combatants had verbally sparred back and forth, but he finally decided it had gone on long enough, so he interrupted by saying "Whoever is responsible or however the arrangements for the mall festivities came about, I'm sure they will be a credit to both of you and all those who assisted you. I now have duties elsewhere and so I wish you a good day."

The shuttle deck had been humming with activity for the last six hours now that more of the population of Drathon III had been arriving to enjoy their tours and receptions aboard the mall ship. The four to five hundred who had been shuttled up from the planet were still only a select group consisting of invited mid-level and minor dignitaries and their families. The planet's general populace wouldn't arrive until after the large reception dinner and dance on the A deck the second night of the mall ship's stay at Drathon III. If Cheng Wong thought she was busy now trying to keep everything running smoothly on the shuttle deck, she would be in for a boatload of work when the bulk of the planet's inhabitants arrived in a matter of thirty-six hours.

"Have all of the passengers disembarked from Shuttle *Neptune*, Lieutenant?" Cheng asked the pilot of the aforementioned shuttle. Having received an answer in the affirmative, she continued, "We need to move it away from the landing area to make room for the final shuttle, the *Mars*. You would think that with a shuttle bay as large as this one, room to land would not be as problematic as it has been."

"I'm sure that is just part of the adjustments we will make for future mass-shuttle arrivals," stated Lieutenant J. G. Valerie Penworth, Cheng's assistant on the shuttle bay. "After all," she continued, "this is only our first port-of-call and the first contingent of multiple arrivals and departures. I'm confident that we will completely work out the bugs by the time the main influx of visitors arrive."

"Thank you for your confidence, Val," returned Cheng. "It's good to know that you are ready for what's coming up the day after tomorrow. We'll need that kind of confidence from the entire shuttle staff but especially from those with command responsibilities like yourself."

"We'll make it work, ma'am," came the quick response from Valerie.

The evening of the grand dinner/dance reception went off without a hitch, much to the relief of everyone in security. The visitors reacted with awe and surprise. There were some who found it a bit disconcerting, but as they became acclimated to it, they became increasingly fascinated by it.

Imagine eating dinner, dancing, and strolling about literally among the stars, with no obstruction to your view while exposed visually to the vacuum of space wearing no protective gear. That takes a few minutes to get your head around.

Chairman Hillian said in his after-dinner speech, "The thrill and awe that fills me at being present to see such a fantastic spectacle as this 'A,' or 'Atmospheric,' deck can hardly be expressed in words. 'Wow' seems such a short and inadequate word to use, but WOW!"

The crowd erupted in thunderous applause and laughter at the chairman's candid comment.

The buffet dinner had been exquisite in its quality and abundance. The main dish of rump of Goldo Beast, from the Keplar 1647 system and the planet Sarnvar, proved to be the gastronomical delight of the evening. It was delicately spiced with a wonderful mildly sweet juiciness.

The music provided for dancing came from three different planets. Ambassador Callurran's home world of Saffo V showcased it's melodic and subtly rhythmic style of dance music. The host world of Drathon III entertained the partygoers with their unique brand of electronic music called "Shwem." And, of course, the earth delighted everyone with a jazz trio and an appeal to the young and young-at-heart with a raucous rock band.

The captain and crew of the Starship *Cosmic Mall* couldn't have been happier with the results.

Keanyn, Mac, and Grannison could now relax somewhat and actually enjoy, to a degree, the remaining eight days of their visit to Drathon III. The same could not be said of Stenn, ND, and Robert Porter, or anyone else from security. They couldn't afford to let their collective guard down for a minute.

If anyone was planning to thwart the operations of the mall starship, the continued vigilance of its entire security team may well have caused the saboteurs to postpone or alter their plans. In any case, the initial visit of the mall to Drathon III Eridea was a resounding success, as were its next two ports-of-call.

This success was the topic of much conversation throughout the Legion and a large number of naysayers concerning the earth project began to speak more favorably about it. There was still a lot of debate and complaint directed against the earth in general and the mall starship in particular, but it was now coming from a smaller group of people.

They were about to dock at their fourth planet, Janos in the Ursa Major system. A comfortable but efficient pattern had now developed by this time and the three months that the mall starship had been operating had proved to be a very pleasant experience, not only for the visiting shoppers but the crew of the ship and the mall personnel as well.

Once they had docked successfully at Janos, Captain Mathews, Science Officer McCardle Stinson, Commander Grannison Loche, and Robert Porter, were having coffee in the officers' mess and discussing the progress of the mission to that point.

"Since you three are all on the bridge when the initial VIP entourage arrives at the mall, I've gotten to experience their amazement, at least in the last two planetary visits," said

Robert. "They are often speechless. But their appreciation can clearly be seen on their faces and especially in their eyes."

The four of them were sitting at one of the circular tables in the mess, which had a gourmet kitchen with a first-class bakery from which came the most delicious, frosted cinnamon rolls in the entire galaxy. That is what the four of them were currently enjoying along with the best Lindovan coffee from the bean brew houses of Gwindor in the Keplar Four system.

Mac broke the congenial silence by saying "Mmm, that frosting is delectable, and I so hate to disturb this moment, but I feel the need to remind you that we are barely through one-fourth of this mission and there is still plenty of time for something to go wrong."

"Leave it up to a woman to look on the dark side of an otherwise smooth and positive situation," stated Keanyn who was especially annoyed at being interrupted as he ate a second cinnamon roll. "We are aware of the dangers that may still be lurking out there," he continued. "But can't we at least enjoy a few minutes of stress-free peace?"

Grannison added his comment, "I fully sympathize with you, Captain, but Mac's right. We can't get side-tracked from our watchfulness. No matter how good that deviation might taste." As he said this, he was licking the remnants of frosting and cinnamon from his upper lip and mustache.

"You're right, of course, Commander," agreed Keanyn. "We've been so busy and any time for a break has been practically nonexistent. I was trying to eke out a tiny bit of R-and-R. Then when I saw my favorite cinnamon rolls, I lost my focus for a minute. Let's get back to the point at hand."

Robert returned to the conversation. "I was talking to

Stenn yesterday, and he said that the lack of any activity by our enemies made him more on-edge and the need for vigilance was more vital."

Another matter that had affected their suspicions was Ambassador Callurran and his activities. He was not as scrutinized as before. Since no overtures of sabotage had occurred and the ambassador himself was not exhibiting any behavior beyond normal, he was being treated as if he had nothing to do with any ill will directed toward them.

It was the second evening of the VIP visit from Janos, and that meant the grand reception on the A deck. The captain, Mac, and Ambassador Callurran were always present at this function, with others from the bridge and mall staffs alternating their appearances. Tonight's festivities would be attended by Chief Computer Systems Officer Lindsey Thompson and Assistant Navigator Edward Butler from the bridge officers as well as Terrance Mckendric, head manager of Davidson's Sporting Goods Emporium, and Rolock Winduru from Delfine, who managed the delightfully serendipitous Adventures for Sale, where you could buy an adventure on any of three different planets in the Alpha Centauri system. These adventures included everything from flying (under your own power) to a safari that hunted dinosaurs. Saffaw was also there as he hardly ever missed an opportunity for free food and fun (not to mention a chance to increase his financial estate by making "new friends"). It goes without saying that Stenn and Robert Porter would be making frequent check-ins.

The banquet and entertainment had gone off beautifully, and the experience of the three previous visits was becoming evident by the smoothness with which the events were unfolding. The roughly six hundred individuals present on the A deck were enjoying after dinner drinks and stimulating conversations ranging from the uniqueness of the Atmospheric deck to the mission of the mall starship itself. There were, of course, any number of private and personal conversations taking place from business arrangements to holiday plans.

The VIPs from Janos were mingling with the other guests in small groups of three or four and the bridge attendees were either a part of those small groups or speaking with close friends they had made on the ship.

One of these was Captain Keanyn Mathews who had been approached by Robert Porter with a slightly concerned look on his face. He had just entered the A deck on one of his frequent visits and had immediately approached the captain. He spoke in a soft whisper, leaning into Keanyn's ear, and said, "I don't think that it is anything to get too excited about, Captain, but as I was on my way here, I stopped by the A deck control room to have a quick look in and found that the code for the locking mechanism seems to have been changed. Since that is something we have done from time to time for security purposes, I didn't think too much of it except for the fact that, as head of security, I was not informed nor did I authorize it. I thought that since I was coming here in the first place, I would ask you if you had authorized the change rather than use my comm device."

The captain's reply was "I neither authorized nor knew of any such change, Robert. Did you not try to talk to Chief Stanfield? I believe he is manning the control room. Perhaps Stenn or ND made the adjustment."

Robert Porter was beginning to look more apprehensive as he shook his head and said, "I couldn't rouse the Chief since you have to punch the locking code to open the comm into the control room. I didn't have the code. Besides, I had just spoken to Stenn and he never mentioned anything about the locking code, which he most certainly would have done due to the fact that I had just told him that I was going to check on the control room."

The captain now had a similar look of apprehension as he looked directly into Robert's eyes and said, "I don't like where this is headed. I don't like it one bit! Use your comm and tell Stenn to meet you and me at the control room ASAP!"

"At once, Captain!" came Robert's reply and he quickly turned and walked as fast as he dared, without alarming any of the other guests, toward the exit of the A deck.

Keanyn took just a minute to excuse himself to the Janos VIPs for his departure, citing necessary command business and followed Robert at a similar quick, but not panicked, pace. It took him less than a minute and a half to reach the control room door, where Robert was talking excitedly to an obviously nervous Stenn.

"If no one with the authority or ability to alter the door codes is responsible for this lock out, then how did this happen?" queried Robert.

Stenn was pacing back and forth, which made Keanyn all the more alarmed as Stenn was the last person to exhibit anything close to distress. Stenn suddenly stopped pacing and stared with a look of focused concentration at the control room door and said, "What about Chief Stanfeld? Isn't he supposed to be in there manning the control board for the A deck? Hasn't he contacted you about the locking code malfunctioning?"

"As I told the Captain, we can't communicate with anyone in the control room unless we enter the code, and the Chief had made no attempts to contact us! He's the first one I tried to contact after I found out that no one had authorized a change in the door code," said Stenn. "There have been no replies to my frequent attempts to contact him."

Keanyn jumped into the conversation. "This is getting more alarming by the second. Gentlemen, we must get into that control room or who knows what kind of calamity we're facing. It seems that our feared sabotage has taken place despite our vigilance, and I fear that the consequences could be far worse than any we might have anticipated."

As he spoke, a dark, imminent foreboding began forming in each of their minds. Would the dissenters of the earth's mission be so malicious as to cause the death of hundreds of innocent individuals? Their suspicions concerning the possible sabotage had not risen to the mass murder of so many. If someone from such a group of terrorists now had control of the functioning of the A deck, the lives of the six hundred plus, currently enjoying a wonderful evening of socializing, could be snuffed out in a matter of seconds.

Keanyn looked at the two security professionals and asked, "Is there an override for the locking mechanism?"

It was Stenn who answered. "Yes, but both Robert and I have already tried it, and you can see how successful it was. Whoever is behind this has thoroughly planned it to the last degree."

"We do have one last option," said Robert. "We can use force and break the lock by cutting through it with a Drumarion laser torch. It's the only laser tool that is powerful and precise enough to surgically cut through the locking mechanism without interfering with the anti-tampering devices inside the locks."

Captain Keanyn Mathews was immediately on his comm. device and calling for help. "Stokes, I need you at the A deck control room with a Drumarion laser torch ASAP!"

"I'll be there in two shakes of an Androvian Sand Lizard's tail!" came the chief engineer's reply.

"Make it one and a half," came the captain's retort.

In just over three minutes, Stokes Davis was there with the tools needed. How he had gotten there so quickly from engineering was a mystery, but Stokes knew the ship inside and out and was aware of many shortcuts from one part of it to another; he could arrive anywhere in record time.

As the last tumblers fell from the locking mechanism, the four men manually pushed open the control room door and ventured inside to view a surprisingly neat and clean interior. There was but one small section that was out of order and that was the prone body of Chief Stanfield on the floor in front of the main control panel. The only other anomaly was a light flashing numerical digits in descending order.

"Is Chief Stanfield all right?" asked Robert after the captain had checked for his vital signs.

"His breathing is a bit shallow, but his pulse is steady. He's probably going to have a nasty concussion but, otherwise, all right. Stenn, call for a medic to get him to sick bay."

Stenn put the order into action and said that Dr. Karushkin would be there as quickly as possible, but that they had a much more pressing problem in regard to the flashing digital light. His words sent a rush of fear through them all.

"That is a countdown to the disabling of the A deck and the fail-safe is not functioning!"

Keanyn stared in shocked disbelief, then looked at Stenn and said, "Are you saying that the atmospheric walls are going to shut down in—" he tilted his head and looked around Robert to get a clear view of the timer readout and continued "—eleven minutes and twelve seconds? There are over six hundred people on that deck, and eleven minutes isn't enough time to get even a hundred of them out of there!"

Stenn looked at the captain with a hopeless expression on his face and in a resigned voice said, "This is worse than I ever could have imagined."

"I for one will not take this lying down," stated Robert with an angrily determined countenance. "We must, at least, get the Janovian VIPs and those of our command staff out of the A deck, and if I can enlist the aid of the three of you, I think we can accomplish that task."

The three others were only too ready to comply, and Stenn was once again himself and was galvanized for action. He was also thinking much more clearly as he said, "We need to be organized by being assigned to help specific groups of individuals or we'll fail."

"I agree," said Robert. "Captain, would you please round up as many of the command staff and medical personnel as you can? Stokes, please get to as many of your engineering staff as you can find in this limited amount of time. Stenn, you and I will gather all of the VIPs and as many women and children that we can get to. The challenge will be to keep from starting a panic. If that happens, no one will get out. Not even us."

It took them less than a minute to get to the A deck, which they entered at a quick but not alarming speed. Keanyn found all but two of the sixteen members from the bridge as well as one of the nurses from sick bay. Stokes proved the most successful as he collected all of the thirteen from engineering who were at the function. Robert and Stenn found twelve of the fourteen-member VIP entourage from the planet, and Stenn noticed Mac and Edward Butler were near the opposite wall, and by the time he got there, they had been joined by Nurse Patsy Tulliver and one of the VIPs, Beliorn Siff, the Minister of Finance on Janus.

"Has anyone seen Ambassador Callurran?" asked Keanyn of Janus' Prime Minister Louwdoaren.

"Why, yes" was his reply. "He was called to deal with a small diplomatic problem that had developed on the shuttle deck only a few minutes before you arrived, Captain."

Alarm bells were going off in Keanyn's head at this statement, and the old suspicions concerning the ambassador began creeping in again. He'd have to deal with those later. By his watch, which had been synchronized with the timer counting down in the control room, they had barely four minutes left before the atmospheric walls collapsed, leaving all breathing entities at the mercy of the vacuum of outer space, where no mercy could be expected.

Meanwhile, on the opposite side of the deck, Stenn had reached the small group of Mac, Edward, Patsy, and Minister Siff, but by the time he had convinced the minister of their predicament, they had less than two minutes to evacuate the deck. As he noticed the seemingly vast distance to the exit, and the sea of people between them and that exit, he knew they wouldn't make it. As he feverishly panned through his mind to find an alternative, he remembered a detail from an instructional talk he had attended concerning the Atmospheric deck. Something about when the walls are retracted, they (or the atmosphere) slide into a four-and-a-half-foot-deep storage chamber that sits between the inner and outer layers of the disc. When the disc is returned to its position under the horizontal shaft, it connects with an airlock chamber at the bottom attachment to the central base, from which a corridor leads to gain access into the ship itself. This airlock access to the atmospheric storage chamber allows for maintenance and repairs to be carried out.

Stenn hoped that if the five of them could slip into that storage chamber as the walls were retracting, they might have a chance to survive and make their way to the airlock. The atmosphere would be heavy, and they would not be able to stand up, but they should be able to get there if they moved slowly and breathed shallowly. He quickly explained this to the others in about thirty seconds and, though they were understandably skeptical, they knew they had no other choice.

When his watch showed three seconds left, Stenn motioned for them to quickly hit the floor and get as close to the edge as they could. They immediately complied, and as the walls retracted, they felt an oppressive heaviness as each of them slipped into what they hoped was not the void of deep space.

Meanwhile, Keanyn, Robert, and Stokes Davis had managed to get the bridge members and the two from sick bay, the thirteen Janovian VIPs, and the thirteen from engineering out of the A deck and safely into the main corridor that led to the shuttle bay and mall with just over two minutes to spare.

"Did anyone get the children out?" said Keanyn in an excited and nervous voice. "Does anyone know where any of them were on that deck?" His voice was now filled with consternation as he and the rest were in horror at the thought of any of the youngsters becoming victims to the sudden depletion of the air they needed to live.

Nurse Kimberly Richards began sobbing at the prospect of such an atrocity. Between her cries, she managed to get out a statement to the effect that she had seen the small group of children enjoying having their faces painted by one of the singers from the choral group that had performed earlier in the evening.

"Where exactly, nurse?" said Robert in a near panicked voice. He added, "Were they close enough to the exit that we might still be able to go back in there and get them out?"

"I'm not sure," came her reply as fresh tears streamed down her face. "I think you would need to have a pretty clear path to them and back out if you were to do it in time."

Robert said, "It's worth a try," and he moved to the door. Just as he reached for the door's access button, it opened, and all fifteen of the children who had been on the deck were being rapidly escorted out by a flushed but determined ND.

Robert looked at her incredulously and with obvious relief. "I thought you had gone to check on the security at the mall. How did you manage to get here and know the dilemma we were facing?"

She had gathered back her composure and stated, with a tone of supreme coolness, "I have made it a habit to monitor all the communications between the heads of security during the major functions of our planetary visits. When I heard you, Robert, communicate to Stenn about the security breach at the A deck control room, I immediately made my way to the deck to see what I could do to help. When I also heard your plans to gather certain groups of individuals, I knew you would have difficulty getting them together. Then, when I saw my son, Stenn, head for the other side of the room, I felt it my duty to round up the children and as many of their parents as I could find. Fortunately, the children were all in one group, with three or four of their parents at the face-painting booth. I managed to grab one or two more of their parents as I was directing the children toward the exit. There are five mothers and two fathers with us, but I am afraid many of these children are going to be orphaned."

Keanyn looked suddenly panicked as he noted. "When

I saw Stenn suddenly depart from our group, I assumed he was going to look for children. Where did he go, ND?"

Her face fell as she showed a rare emotional countenance and quietly stated, "I saw him head toward the far side of the room from the exit and noticed that Mac and Edward Butler were over there with a couple of others in conversation. If his intention was to inform them of the situation and get them out, I'm afraid he probably would not have had time to accomplish it." She lowered her head as her golden/black hair fell in front of her face and a low sob escaped.

Keanyn was stunned as he cried out, "Mac and Edward? I wondered where they were when I couldn't find them with the rest of the bridge crew. I'd hoped that they left to attend to some duties or just to get some quiet time. We need our science officer desperately, and what am I going to say to Grannison?"

They didn't have much time to contemplate this as the sound in the corridor became suddenly still and the ominous noise of rushing wind followed by a loud *THWACK!* could be felt as well as heard.

They all knew what that meant, and that the instantaneous loss of hundreds of lives had just occurred.

Chapter 14

Shutdown

Grannison Loche, who was in command of the bridge, had been feeling increasingly uneasy during the last hour. That was strange seeing that everything on the bridge was running quite smoothly. His uneasiness did not stem from his responsibilities as commander but had to do with matters outside of his control. He hadn't heard from the captain nor Robert or Stenn for a little over an hour, and one of them would usually give him periodic rundowns of the activities on the A deck when the reception dinner was taking place.

He had attended only one of the four receptions that had taken place thus far and found it to be rather boring. Grannison was not much of a social animal outside of those he worked closely with. Add to that the fact that his idea of excitement consisted of piloting fighters, shuttles, and the amazing vessel he currently occupied, attending a social function full of political, bureaucratic, and any number of diva-like personalities was not his cup of tea.

He had not tried to contact any of the three previously mentioned individuals because he had been especially busy with his responsibilities on the bridge. His time had also been taken up with a small contingency of Janovian visitors who had wanted a closer look at the bridge operations.

Suddenly the voice of Captain Mathews came over Grann's personal comm saying "Commander Loche, we have a critical situation on the A deck, and I need you to calmly—and I can't stress 'calmly' enough—inform the bridge crew of the very real possibility of all of you witnessing hundreds of bodies floating into outer space in the next few minutes."

It was everything he could do to keep from shouting back "Are you crazy, Captain?" but Grannison sensed the seriousness and near-panic that Keanyn was feeling, and after a few seconds gathering his nerves and suppressing the shock, he quietly asked Keanyn, "What happened?"

Keanyn hurriedly replied, "There isn't much time, but the A deck controls have been compromised and the fail-safes were overridden, making for the failure of the atmospheric walls in less than ninety seconds. We've gotten out as many as we possibly could. I'm afraid that among those we weren't able to get to included Edward and Mac." He paused as emotion was beginning to overwhelm him, but he managed to control it, and with a voice heavy with grief and apology, he said, "I am so very sorry, Grann. If we had had more time, they probably would have made it. Stenn went to get them, but they were just too far from the exit for the time remaining. I'm afraid that it means we have lost Stenn as well."

There was another longer pause as both Grannison and

Keanyn tried to steady themselves. Keanyn finished with one last statement. "I have to break off. We must see to the survivors. I'll get back with you soon."

Grannison was rubbing his eyes on his sleeve as he opened the comm to the public-address mode. The bridge crew had sensed that something was very wrong and turned their eyes toward their commander as he addressed them.

"There is no good way to tell you this, but the captain just informed me that the A deck walls have been compromised and will be shutting down in less than a minute. Be prepared to witness a horrendous sight. JA, contact the shuttle bay and have Lieutenant Cheng prepare to launch as many shuttles as she can in order to pick up some six hundred passengers! If she questions you, tell her that it is a direct order from me!"

"Aye, aye, sir," came J. A. Philpot's reply.

The crew had no time to absorb Grannison's statement before warning lights began to go off all over the bridge. Twenty seconds later, the sound of the atmospheric walls retracting followed by the bodies of over six hundred people floating into deep space provided a scene none of them would ever forget.

"JA, has Cheng responded yet?" shouted Grannison over the cacophony of voices reverberating throughout the bridge.

JA shook his head to rid it of the horrible sight he had just witnessed and answered Grannison with "She seems confused with all of the warnings going off and no explanations as to why."

Grannison grabbed the comm mic from JA's trembling hands and spoke into it. "Lieutenant Wong. We have an emergency from the A deck. It has malfunctioned and retracted, leaving some six hundred exposed to the vacuum of space. We need to get all shuttles out there as quickly as possible. We must salvage as many bodies as possible in order to give them a proper burial."

Cheng Wong came on the comm unit saying "I fully agree, Commander Loche."

"There's a lot of confusion here as we were treated to the full view of the atrocity," stated Grann.

"I'm sorry, sir," Cheng replied. "We have seven shuttle craft prepared for immediate departure. They will all launch within the minute. What are the chances any of them can survive even that long?"

Grannison said, "You've probably heard the same theories I have, Cheng. Nothing's been proven."

"Mac has done some work in that area. Has she offered any comments on the chances of survival?" commented Cheng.

Grannison hung his head and gave a long sigh before responding to Cheng's question. "I'm afraid that she has already received an answer as she was one of those on the A deck. My brother, Edward, was another." It took a monumental effort for him to keep from falling apart in total grief, but he remained looking straight ahead into the comm screen.

Cheng gave a sharp intake of breath then covered her face. The tears streamed through her hands. She got her composure back as quickly as she could and said to Grannison with sobs still in her voice, "I don't know what to say. This is worse than I could have imagined."

Grannison Loche could not respond as his emotions had finally overtaken him.

It was now three days since the catastrophic events on the A deck. The shuttle bay had continuously been employed in the retrieval of the bodies, and Lieutenant

Cheng Wong was coordinating the rescue efforts. They were still assessing the body count, but they had actually rescued a dozen or more who were still alive. They were among those who were standing near the edge of the 'A' deck next to the wall.

A group of officers from the bridge and engineering along with several from security were in the officers' mess discussing the future of their mission.

"I'm not going to take this defeat as the end of our mission!" stated Robert Porter vehemently. "These low-life cowards that instigated this atrocity will be caught and, if I have anything to do with it, they will die for this." As head of security, he felt responsible for allowing it to happen. He should have been able to discover their plot and thwart it.

Keanyn spoke. "I understand your feelings, Lieutenant Commander, but as far as the continuation of our mission is concerned, there has been no decision to scrub it completely. We have just been put on temporary shutdown, pending investigations. I have requested that we be allowed to conduct our own internal investigation. I argued that we had already been looking into the sabotage possibility and had uncovered a lot of clues and that we were here at the scene of the crime and have firsthand knowledge of the events."

"Did that convince them?" asked Dooley Paxton, who had come over from the *Gator* as had Zach Demopolis from the *Crockett*.

"It softened them up a bit so that when General Beckton chimed in with his support of us, they reluctantly agreed."

Grannison, who was continuing to mourn the loss of his half-brother, Edward, said, "You and the general have formed a bond since the Swamp Maneuver. It's good to have him as an ally. As I understand it, Captain, he helped you convince the council that you deserved to win the competition, even though you stretched the rules a bit. I only wish that Edward and Mac could have defeated the A deck disaster as well."

Keanyn put a sympathetic arm around Grannison's shoulder and said, "Altering the rules was a part of our plan, but it didn't include any real contact with alligators. If Captain Paxton hadn't been part of our group, I would, most assuredly, not be here today." He looked at Dooley and gave him a wink and a smile as the captain of the *Gator* smiled back at him and said, "I was more than happy to lend a hand. I just didn't know it would end up being my whole arm."

The occupants of the mess hall smiled and a few chuckled, and that seemed to bring them out of the funk they had been in the last three days. Leave it to Dooley Paxton to brighten the mood.

Lieutenant Cheng Wong and Chief Engineer Stokely Davis entered the officers' mess at this point, and Cheng said, "We've got a final body count from the A deck event, as they're officially calling it. We recovered four hundred and eighty-nine bodies, including one of the fourteen we rescued alive. Her internal organs just couldn't overcome exposure to the vacuum of space any longer."

"I've been intrigued by the fact that some fourteen, now thirteen, individuals were able to survive being thrust out into deep space," broke in Stokes. "I was especially interested in the fact that all of them had been standing quite near to the outer edge of the deck near the wall. The two or three who have revived enough to speak have said that they were standing very close to what appeared to be vents in the floor along the edge of the deck. If that is the case with all of the survivors, then I might be able to put forth a possible reason for their remaining alive despite the harsh conditions into which they were thrust."

Dr. Karushkin, who had entered the officers' mess some fifteen minutes earlier, spoke up. "Chief Davis, as a medical man, I would be highly interested in your thoughts on this. As you know, I and my staff have been working feverishly, tending to the survivors. The three that have become conscious will soon be joined by six or seven of the others. The other three still alive are in very serious condition to the point that one, if not all of them, will sustain moderate to severe brain damage. So how do you think they survived in the first place, Chief?"

Stokes answered, "Those vents that were mentioned as being near the edge of the deck floor are actually retrieving portals for any of the atmosphere that doesn't quite get pulled back into the storage chamber under the deck plating where the walls are stored when not in use. If enough of that residual atmosphere is retained on the outer edge of the deck flooring, then it might be possible for someone to be encompassed in a cocoon-like atmosphere that would gradually dissipate but might keep them alive for a brief period of time."

"I don't pretend to know the science behind all of that," said the captain, "but if what you say is true, Stokes, it provides a plausible explanation for the survivors."

At this point, Cheng interjected. "In addition to the body count, I was also going to tell you that Mac, Edward, and Stenn were not found among the bodies. Now that I've heard Chief Davis' explanation about those that survived, I wonder about our three fellow officers. They were, supposedly, near the edge of the platform. Could they have survived in some kind of cocoon as well?"

Stokes Davis rubbed his hands together, smiling, and said, "I think I have an idea about that as well."

The others looked at the chief engineer with keen anticipation. Dr. Karushkin spoke up, saying "I suspect that as chief engineer, you have some specific knowledge of the atmospheric deck that the rest of us are not privy to."

"That's correct, Doctor," said Stokes. "Even more importantly, I happen to know that Stenn possesses the same knowledge."

"And how is that?" declared Keanyn.

Stokely Davis rested his arms on the table where they were seated and stated very clearly, "Since the A deck was one of the prime areas targeted for possible sabotage, Stenn told me that he wanted to know as much as he could about the operation of the mechanisms for the deck. I approved him to have access to any of the instructional lectures that were designed for the engineering department's eyes and ears only."

He continued, "While he did not attend all the lectures, he did attend one on the workings of the A deck when it was deployed for use and then retracted."

"And just what would he have learned from that lecture?" questioned Commander Grannison Loche. "You referred to Stenn in the present tense. Was that on purpose or just a mistake?"

A commotion began to arise among the small group gathered around the table. Before it could get to the level of total confusion, Stokes held his hands up and gestured for the excited group to calm down so they could listen to his further explanation.

"This is an idea that has only dawned on me as we were talking about the tragedy and those few that have survived because of being near the edge. I began to realize that if Stenn recalled that information and quickly prepared the others, there was a possibility they could have survived the sudden elimination of those protective walls by virtually throwing themselves down toward the very edge of the platform just as the wall was retreating into the storage area, and Stenn's group would have been drawn into it as well!"

Cheng Wong spoke. "But it's been three days. Can we be certain that they will still be alive?"

Stokes was now grabbing his comm device and speaking into it. "Ensign Halliday, get three others from engineering and equip yourselves with the gear necessary to enter the A deck storage compartment. And Ensign, this is no maintenance operation. This is an emergency. Lives are involved! I'll brief you when we meet at the storage-bay entrance in five minutes."

"Right on it, Chief!" was the instant reply from the ensign.

The three captains, Mathews, Demopolis, and Paxton, along with Grannison and Dr. Karushkin, rapidly followed Stokes Davis out of the officers' mess toward the storage compartment. On the way, Stokes explained the reason why they were in such a hurry.

"I don't know why I didn't think of this earlier. I guess I was caught up in all of the grief," Stokes said. "If Stenn and the others did what I think they did, then they would have been swept into the storage area by the force of the walls as it was being sucked into it. Aside from that putting them into a very tight area only four and a half feet tall, the atmosphere that exists in that chamber, while breathable, is heavier than our bodies are used to. If they were to make it all the way across the deck to the maintenance portal, they would have to breathe very shallowly and move very slowly so as not to become oppressively fatigued, black out, and eventually, die. I'm banking on Stenn remembering that from the lecture and moving and breathing very slowly. That would account for them still being in there even after three days. Alive, I hope."

They now arrived at the door to the A deck maintenance portal almost simultaneously with the four properly suited individuals from engineering. Stokes took charge and donned the extra suit that was brought for him. He then led them into the A deck storage compartment.

The five searchers turned on their helmet lights as well as two strong flash beams they had brought along. Once they were all in the massive, but low ceiling, atmospheric storage area, Chief Davis turned to the other four and said, "I am going to turn on my mic to loudspeaker mode. The rest of you keep yours on person-to-person comm. If we all start calling for them at once, it will be too confusing."

Since they were properly equipped, they could move at a normal pace and not be hampered by the heavy atmosphere.

Stokes called up the schematic for the storage area on his multi-functional comm unit and decided to move to the left-hand corridor, which proceeded in the general direction of the last known position on the A deck where Stenn's group had been seen.

"While we can move faster than they can, there is a maze of corridors here, and we could easily miss them if we are not methodical and observant," said Stokes. "I am going to make my first call for them. After I'm done, be very quiet for several seconds so that we can hear if they make a reply."

They were moving in a crouched position at a steady rate, though the breather modules strapped on to their backs did hinder them to a degree. They had gone about one hundred to one hundred and twenty feet into the corridor when Stokes made his first attempt to contact Stenn's party with a fairly loud shout of "Stenn and Mac, if you are in here, try to let us know. Don't shout, but if you can, bang on something metal."

Everything was quiet for a good ten seconds as they waited for a response. None was forthcoming.

Stokes tried two more times without results, and their hope, which was fairly high when they entered the storage corridor, waned with every silent response.

They had just rounded a jog in the corridor when Stokes said, "I'm going to try one more time along this track we've been taking, and if the response is the same, we'll stop and decide to change direction or keep going in this one."

They all agreed, and Stokes repeated his message a fourth time. They waited nearly twice as long for an answer but got none, and with concerned faces, gathered in a small circle to discuss their options. Stokes started by asking for opinions. Ken Dalany, one of the engineers in charge of the trilliatide fuel mix, suggested that if they backtracked to a main cross corridor, they could get to the intersecting main corridor that went straight through to the other side of the A deck. He was reasoning that that was a logical path for the lost party to take as it would be a direct route out. He had just finished pointing this out when Ensign Marough Verellian, a Kinip from Garsden, said, "Be quiet! I think I heard something!"

Stokes quickly pulled the ensign closer and said, "What did it sound like?"

Marough's response was "It certainly sounded like someone banging on a metal pipe to me, Chief."

As they stooped there in stunned silence, the unmistakable sound of metal on metal reverberated through the corridor, and Stokes shouted, "We hear you. We are in corridor L-Two, is that where you are? One knock for yes and two knocks for no."

It took about five seconds, but the sound of a single knock rang joyously in their ears.

They proceeded as quickly and safely as they could up the corridor until they saw the light of one of their flash beams reflect off what appeared to be a shiny metal object lying in the corridor. As they adjusted their focus on the form lying next to what proved to be a silver belt buckle, it moved, and a low groan emerged from it. They had found the missing group of bridge and sick bay members.

An involuntary joyful noise came from Stokes Davis' lips. He could not contain his relief as he rushed to the fallen form and found it to be Stenn. Stenn was very weak but did muster up a small smile to greet the rescuers. The rest of the time was spent by the four rescuers gathering up the four other survivors. They shared their refreshing mix of oxygen, and within five minutes, they were on their way out of the corridor to exit the atmospheric deck.

"Even though I knew about the possibility of slipping into the storage vault for the A deck, I wasn't prepared for the stifling closeness of the atmosphere in such a confined space," remarked Stenn the morning after his rescue. He, Mac, Edward, and two others were all resting comfortably in sick bay under the careful watch of Dr. Karushkin.

Stenn continued his recounting of their harrowing experience. "It's not like normally walking from a large auditorium into a smaller room. Yes, the air may be a bit more stuffy, but it's not debilitating. I mean, the air was so heavy that it made moving, even at a snail's pace, agonizing."

Nurse Patsy Tulliver added her recollection at this point. "We would pass out frequently at first, and this would relax our bodies so that we would recover fairly quickly, but it took us a while before we learned how to pace ourselves and stop passing out. We had to move extremely slowly and stop moving altogether for several minutes at a time in order to make any kind of consistent progress."

"Even so," broke in Mac, "we figured that by the end of the first day, we had only gotten some fifty yards closer to the access chamber." She added another fact. "Stenn had, fortunately, drawn a copy of the schematic of the storage area and had memorized it so that he had a good idea which corridors to take for the most direct route to the exit."

Stenn spoke again. "It still required us making several changes of direction, and if I had forgotten or miscalculated any of that schematic, you might never have found us," he paused before finishing his comment with the words "alive at any rate."

"I'm just very glad that both you and I had studied those schematics which helped bring about this happy solution," Chief Stokes Davis chimed in.

Captain Keanyn Mathews spoke out with a wide grin on his face. "What's more, I am so happy to see you have recovered well, Minister Siff, and once again, I am deeply sorry for this disastrous occurrence and hope there are no hurt feelings between our two worlds."

The Janovian Minister of Finance had a stern look as he commented. "While I understand your unfortunate predicament, Captain, I also feel that you could have had a better handle on the situation. It is my understanding you had been suspecting that some act of sabotage was imminent. It appears that you wasted a lot of money in a futile attempt to thwart the sabotage and, still more funds, in whatever attempts you will make to appease we Janovians. You must understand. This has damaged our relationship."

As finance minister, it was natural that Beliorn Siff would look at the situation from a monetary point of view.

Keanyn tried to calm the minister's ire by taking responsibility for the disaster, concluding with "As bad as the loss of that amount of revenue is, our mission is in grave jeopardy, in addition to the harm it has caused between our two worlds. And for that, I am profoundly sorry."

Minister Siff was moved by Captain Mathew's forthright statement, and his following comments evidenced his more congenial attitude.

"Captain, it is always refreshing to see someone take responsibility for an unfortunate occurrence. Your candor will go a long way in neutralizing the offense some have taken over this incident. I do have to admit that I would hate to see your mission terminated. I was rather enjoying myself up until the disaster."

"I assure you, Minister," promised Keanyn, "We will do our utmost to rectify this unfortunate incident and normalize our relationship with Janos."

"I appreciate that, Captain. And as for myself, we can conduct our business normally from this point forward."

With that possible crisis averted, the conversation turned back to the five A deck survivors.

Edward Butler spoke, saying "I can't ever remember being so restricted in my movements and yet still able to function. It was like trying to walk with a one-hundred-pound weight strapped to your back."

Stenn quickly moved into his security mode as he asked, "What's being done to find the perpetrators of this infamous act of terrorism. I can't tell you how frustrated and angry I am."

"The answer is everything possible!" stated Robert Porter as he entered sick bay just as Stenn was making his embittered remark. "We are looking at any and all scenarios, but we haven't nailed anything down."

"Well, step it up then!" Stenn shot back irritably.

The entire room became silent at this last rebuke, but the awkward silence was broken by Robert's sarcastic reply. "I'll be sure to see that your mother receives that last statement. She needs to be more concerned over her son's well-being."

Stenn's entire face turned a beet red as he replied, "I don't appreciate your suggestion that my mother doesn't care for my well-being. Besides, you know better than that!"

Mac spoke swiftly from her bedside. "Cut it out, you two! Haven't we been through enough without this petty bickering?"

Both Stenn and Robert looked properly chastised as Stenn said, "Like you, Robert, I am very frustrated over the despicable actions of the saboteurs. But even more so by my inability to prevent it from happening, and that is what prompted my harsh statement. I am sorry."

"No need to apologize, Stenn," said Robert. "After what you have just been through with literally life and death circumstances, your impatience to get to the bottom of this tragic situation is shared by all of us."

Dr. Karushkin entered the room and announced that the thirteen that had survived would all make a fast and nearly full recovery. What problems some would have ranged from memory loss to minor learning disabilities. Also," he said, "of the four hundred and ninety victims, some one hundred and seventeen were part of the mall starship crew."

"Do you mean to say that they were all part of the

military crew of this ship?" queried Grannison. "Were none of them from the mall staff or the diplomatic contingent?"

"I'm sorry, Commander, I used the word crew in too broad of a sense. The breakdown of the deceased was fifty-eight from the military crew, with all but four of them not being officers," stated the doctor. "The four officers consisted of two junior-grade lieutenants from the supply ship, Depot One, and one from the *Crocket*. I'm very sorry for your loss, Captain Paxton. I understand that Lieutenant Kraus was a valued member of your staff."

Dooley Paxton replied in a very subdued tone, "Thank you, Doctor. Indeed, Carl Kraus was an integral part of the *Crocket's* gunnery crew. He trained a number of our young men and women in the defensive aspect of our ship. He will be sorely missed."

After several sympathetic expressions from the others in the room, Doctor Karushkin continued to identify the downed officers from the vicious sabotage attack. "The fourth and final officer was Lieutenant Commander Russell Evans, serving as a direct representative of the Galactic Legion, who boarded the mall starship at our previous port-of-call." Everyone reacted to this bit of information with everything from confusion to outright shock.

Keanyn spoke up first by saying "In the short time he was with us, he proved to be a very congenial fellow. I think he was very aware that as a representative of the Legion, he needed to tread carefully in order to gain the confidence of the officers and crew."

The doctor finished up his account of the A deck victims by noting that the fifty-nine others connected to the ship were employees of the mall stores and sick bay staff, which were now numbered at twenty-one with the loss of three from the tragedy.

Robert Porter now said, "I almost forgot why I came here in the first place. If Stenn and Mac are up to it, I need to speak with them and Captain Mathews, Commander Loche, and Lieutenant Wong as well as ND, who are on their way. If the good doctor will permit, I must kindly ask the rest of you to leave while we discuss some important matters."

Doctor Karushkin looked sternly at the head of ship security and then toward the two of his patients Robert had named and said, "Mr. Porter, I will allow you just ten minutes to conduct your business with my patients. They have not recovered sufficiently to the point of full participation in their duties. Keep your discussions to the facts and try not to waste time with theories and subtexts."

Robert Porter looked concerned and it was also reflected on the faces of the captain and Mac as he replied. "I wouldn't think of jeopardizing the health of Stenn and our chief science officer, Doctor. I will be sure to keep our meeting to the time specified."

"I will hold you to that, Mr. Porter," declared the doctor as he turned a serious look toward Captain Mathews.

When the others had left, and Cheng Wong and ND arrived, Robert called their impromptu meeting to order by saying "We need to discuss the whereabouts and possible involvement of Ambassador Callurran in this terrorist plot, for, it seems to me, he is involved up to his eyeballs."

"The first thing we need to do is find him," said Keanyn. "He hasn't been seen since he was, supposedly, summoned from the A deck shortly before the tragedy."

ND spoke. "Robert and I made sure that an extremely thorough search of this ship was made to find where the ambassador might be hiding, and we turned up nothing. His quarters appeared normal. All of his clothes and personal belongings are still there."

"As impossible as it seems, it appears that the ambassador is not on this ship. Somehow, we weren't able to detect his departure!" noted Robert incredulously.

"That reminds me," said Stenn. "Didn't our stowaway, Salfrod, get onto this ship in a similarly undetected manner?"

Captain Keanyn Mathews sat up and said, "I think we owe Salfrod another friendly visit to see if his memory has been jogged any further so as to help us get to the bottom of this dilemma!"

The previous Stowaway Investigative Team, sans Mac and Stenn, found Dr. Karushkin in his office. He looked up from his review of the A deck survivor records and gave the group a long perusal before cautiously asking "To what do I owe this visit of top brass from this ship? I hope that it is not to ask that I release Mac and Stenn from my watch care, because the records I've just been looking at indicate that they need to remain here in sick bay for at least two more days."

Cheng, ND, Grannison, Robert Porter, and the captain stared back at the doctor with innocent smiles that would fool no one. Captain Keanyn Mathews took the role of spokesman and said, "I assure you, Doctor, that though their presence would greatly facilitate our mission, we are not here to plead the discharge of Mac and/or Stenn."

"That's good to hear, but I am sure your visit is not going to make me happy," said Dr. Karushkin.

"I don't know if our request will make you feel one way or another," stated Keanyn. "We would like another opportunity to talk with Salfrod, if we might."

The good doctor replied, "Seeing as I will be releasing him tomorrow to work under the close supervision of Lieutenant Wong here as part of the shuttle deck crew, I don't think a short session with the five of you would overly tax him."

Captain Mathews looked at Cheng and said, "Did you know about this?"

"I most certainly did not, sir!" came the startled reply of the shuttle bay commander.

The doctor chimed in with an explanation, "I was, in fact, about to communicate my decision to you after I looked over his chart and those of Mac and Stenn."

Keanyn said, "As I am this ship's captain, the assigning of duties must come through me. Why did you think you could assign Salfrod, a stowaway I might add, to an assignment on this starship?"

Doctor Karushkin was not intimidated as he answered, "As his primary doctor, I have the authority to make decisions concerning my patients, including what I would deem necessary for their recovery. While I acknowledge that he is not an official member of this ship's crew, if he could be put in a position to help recover more of his memory, it would be good for him, and it might give us more information. I knew that Salfrod was found on one of the shuttles and that Lieutenant Wong would be an excellent individual to keep an eye on him, therefore I made what I considered to be a medical decision that was within the purview of my authority."

"Did you have any intention of informing the command staff of this starship concerning your decision?" returned the captain.

"Of course, Captain," said Karushkin. "I was going to let you know all of this when I finished up here, but you burst in and I had no time to get the assignment to you."

"Well, now that you've informed me, would you like to know my reply?" said Captain Mathews with little attempt to hide his anger.

"Certainly, Captain," returned the doctor.

"While I applaud your reasoning as to jogging Salfrod's memory, I absolutely deny your claim that it was within the authority you have as his physician to give him an assignment within any part of this vessel! You certainly could have approached me or another member of the command staff with the idea. Then we could have discussed the possibility of implementing it, OR NOT!" returned Keanyn, somewhat hotly.

While the doctor was somewhat taken aback by Keanyn's heated rebuke, it did not prevent him from replying. "Captain Mathews, I do apologize for my presumptuousness, though I assure you I would never have implemented my intention without discussing it with you and getting your approval. I'm sorry that I chose this somewhat inappropriate occasion to inform you of my idea."

"I accept your apology, Doctor, and I do understand your laudable concern for your patient," replied Keanyn. "Though the timing was a bit awkward, I do think there may be some merit to your idea. I can make a more informed decision once we talk with Salfrod again. But first, how do you assess his current condition?"

Doctor Karushkin replied thoughtfully, "I am pleased to report that I have seen a significant improvement in his ability to reason and make cognitive decisions. I would say his maturity level is that of a young teenager, which is a definite improvement from your first discussion with him."

Robert spoke next saying "That's good news, Doctor, but has his memory improved at the same rate?"

"I'm happy to say that his memory has improved, but not at quite the rate as his intelligence. He seems to remember a bit more concerning the activities that occurred just after he arrived in the cockpit of the shuttle where he was found. He still does not remember how he got there in the first place or even how he was on the *Hawk* to begin with." As he finished, he shrugged his shoulders as if to say, *That's the best I can do.*

Robert and Keanyn nodded but it was Grannison that spoke. "Thank you, Doctor. That may be enough for us to get what we want in our conversation with our congenial stowaway."

They entered Salfrod's room to find him up and in the middle of his therapeutic exercises. He immediately stopped when he noticed the rather large group of visitors. He gave them a warm welcoming smile and said, "I am glad to see all of you again, but I didn't think it would be all at once like the last time. I hope that I can think of you, truly, as friends."

His greeting suggested that he had come to understand that their first meeting had not necessarily been the congenial discussion it may have appeared to be.

Keanyn spoke on behalf of the rest when he said, "I do apologize, Salfrod, for the measure of insincerity we had during our first meeting. I hope that Dr. Karushkin explained the reasons for our lack of the friendliest of motives during that visit."

Salfrod's smile was less broad but still sincere as he answered the captain. "As some of my memory and still more of my maturity returned to me, I did express my serious doubts as to the motives of your questioning, but when the good doctor gradually explained the situation to me and revealed that I was, actually, a stowaway on board this vessel, I completely understood the reasons. And now that this tragedy has occurred, I'm surprised that I wasn't under guard and your interview wasn't more suspicious toward me than it had been."

"Dr. Karushkin had explained your condition to us, and we felt that no more precautions needed to be taken," answered Grannison.

Robert Porter said, "We are now glad to see you are feeling better."

Salfrod seemed to be truly genuine as he said, "I was really hoping that, despite the reason I was on your ship in the first place, you would come to the conclusion that I do not continue to wish you, your ship, or its mission any harm, and that I could somehow be your friend."

Cheng spoke up. "When I and one of my shuttle crewmen found you lying just aft of the cockpit in the Solyuz shuttle, we thought that you were dead. And then we found out that you were not on the roster of the ship's crew, it raised a lot of questions that needed immediate answers. When we learned that you survived your blows, we became very anxious to try and get some answers from you."

"I don't think I gave you much to go on from that interview," stated Salfrod.

"On the contrary," disagreed Keanyn. "You gave us at least two very important bits of information that can still prove to be helpful, especially since the catastrophic occurrence on the A deck."

"What could I possibly have said that could help you now?" asked Salfrod.

It was Robert who next spoke. "If you remember, you mentioned that the crew of the ship you came from, the *Hawk*, alluded to the thought that someone they called the ambassador, who seemed to be calling the shots for your mission, and now, the ambassador on this ship, who has direct ties to certain individuals on the *Hawk*, has come up missing. That's just a bit more than a little coincidental, don't you think?"

"Most assuredly it is!" replied Salfrod with an emphatic nod.

If any of the others wondered why Robert was being so free with his information, especially being the head of security, he had a very good reason for being so transparent. He had been keeping a close eye on Salfrod's recovery and had had a number of discussions with Dr. Karushkin concerning it.

He had learned that Salfrod had been more of a pawn rather than a chief player in the sabotage plot. Salfrod was being used for his knowledge of security programming systems and not as a member of a terrorist organization plotting the downfall of the earth's contribution to the Galactic Legion. True, he did have some sympathy toward the discrediting of the *Cosmic Mall,* but most of that feeling had been the result of half-truths and other misinformation directed toward Earth's project.

While that information had helped Robert develop a kinder opinion toward Salfrod, he still needed to hear Salfrod express just exactly how he felt. He now asked him, "Salfrod, I understand that you have been supplying the good doctor here with tidbits of information as your memory has improved. I think we would all be greatly appreciative if you could relate some of it to us at this time."

"I would be happy to tell you anything that has to do with my presence on your ship as well as my motives for being here and how those motives have changed. I'm guessing that is what you specifically want to hear and not just general information," said Salfrod with a knowing gleam in his dark brown eyes that contained the twin pupils particular to Cherillians.

Robert replied, "I believe your recovery is further along

than we thought. I've heard something about your newfound sympathy for this project." As he said this, he used an expansive gesture with his arms to denote the mall starship as "this project."

Salfrod's explanation began with a slightly bowed head to demonstrate the measure of shame he felt for the animosity he'd harbored toward the earth and its contribution. "I am so sorry that I had succumbed to the propaganda that was, and still is, being spewed forth about this remarkable ship. I wanted to see some damage come to the project because I felt that it was an insult to the dignity of the Galactic Legion. Note that I said *some* damage. Not a terrorist plot that would take the lives of hundreds of innocent creatures!" As he said this, he put his head in his hands and began to sob.

Captain Mathews cleared his throat and spoke. "We are all still in a state of shock, Salfrod, but it's good to see that you did not wish any physical harm to come to anyone. But why did you still come to this ship if you weren't in agreement with the plot?"

"That's just it," answered Salfrod. "I was not told of the true nature of the terrorists' intentions when I was transported from the *Hawk*. I thought that I was supposed to gain access to the A deck control room to alter some of the security codes so that access to the A deck would be inhibited in order to hold the VIP entourage from Drathon Three Eridea hostage. There had never been any talk about doing any harm to them or anyone else."

It was Cheng who now asked the question "Then how did you find out about the plot to disable the A deck and kill everyone on it?"

Salfrod's look demonstrated the disgust and horror he had felt when he first heard the cowardly plot. "I hadn't been on the Solyuz shuttle more than a couple of minutes when my contact on this ship showed up. And before you ask, I did not see who or what it was. I had been going through my case of tools that I would need to complete my assignment when whoever it was entered the shuttle and told me not to turn around and look at them because it would be better for the both of us if I couldn't identify them.

"I guess there was a communication breakdown between the leaders of the conspiracy and this liaison, because she—I realize now that my definite impression was that of a female—assumed I knew all of the details of the sabotage. When she disclosed that the programs I would sabotage were the controls for the raising and lowering of the A deck as well as dismantling the fail-safe, it wasn't much of a leap of thought to realize that murder was at the heart of the plot. Upon realizing that, I began to protest pretty forcefully, and when I turned around to confront the liaison, they—or she—knocked me unconscious before I could get a good look at them."

Robert Porter quickly interjected the question, "When you turned around to see this person, did you get an idea of any physical characteristics they may have possessed? I mean size, shape, or even what they were wearing?"

Salfrod was now running his hands through his hair as if he were trying to pull the thoughts from his memory. "All I can recall at this time is the sense of someone large," he said. "Like someone tall and broad. I'm sorry, but that is all I can come up with."

"And you are fairly certain that it was a female?" queried Keanyn as he reminded Salfrod and the others of that detail that had been mentioned earlier.

"Yes, that's right," stated Salfrod.

"Well," noted Grannison, "Those details, though sketchy,

do narrow the field considerably. There are only a limited number of alien species that fit even that sparce a description."

Cheng spoke up next. "Why do you say alien species, Commander? There are a few humans on this vessel that could be described as tall and broad." She looked at Grannison with perplexity.

"I apologize, Lieutenant," said Grannison. "I didn't mean to suggest that any human member of our crew couldn't be involved. I just felt that if Salfrod took note of someone who was particularly large, he probably wasn't speaking about a human, or he might have said a large human. There are several alien races on board whose smallest representative is noticeably larger than the largest human."

Salfrod spoke. "The person was most definitely not human, though I've only just now realized that. By your bringing that point up, it's made it clearer to me that the size of my attacker was definitely taller and bulkier than a human." He looked around a bit sheepishly at everyone as if to apologize for causing any discord.

Robert smiled and patted Salfrod lightly on the shoulder, saying "Don't worry, my friend. That little confrontation has helped you remember a very important detail. We can narrow our search down from nearly everyone on board to, perhaps, just a hundred or so. That will prove to be a tremendous time saver."

"In any case," stated Keanyn, "we still have our work cut out for us. I would like to remind you all that we still need to locate Ambassador Callurran and figure out if or how deeply he is involved in this plot and maintain our vigilance against any further attacks. There are still, probably, members of this murderous plot still aboard this vessel. We need to identify them and dismantle this conspiracy as soon as possible!"

"I might have a line on the possible location of the ambassador," said Grannison. "One of my contacts in the mall told me they saw the ambassador heading toward the Raushdonian pub at about twenty-fifteen. They said there were two other individuals quite close to him. It appeared that they were trying to hurry him along, but they couldn't be sure."

Keanyn and Robert looked up sharply, but it was Cheng who spoke up. "This is very significant," she said. "Did they identify who those two were?"

Grannison replied. "It was difficult to identify them as they wore hoods. But about a half hour later, they came out of the pub, but Callurran never did!"

Robert said, "You know that Saffaw's cousin Hammfrual owns the pub. If he is involved in the sabotage, we need to keep a close eye on him. And possibly Saffaw as well!"

Two days later, Mac, Stenn, and Edward, along with all those who had been rescued from the A deck, were released from Dr. Karushkin's close care. He still cautioned them to take good care of themselves and try not to do too much. Stenn immediately hunted up Robert Porter and his mother to get filled in on what he had missed. Still, they did manage to just pay attention to the doctor's admonition, though they were determined to do what they felt they needed to in order to help bring about a satisfactory conclusion to all this mess.

Acknowledgments

For a first-time author with little to no formal training, I was eager to run practically every new chapter before the eyes of any number of my friends and acquaintances. As you might imagine, there were those who were eager to view them, some who politely complied, and others who thought I was wasting not only my time but theirs as well.

Let me say that I understand every one of you. I was also eager to move forward with this project and, at times, plodded along wondering if it was worth it. Finally, there were moments that I didn't want to do it and could just as easily have thrown it away.

For those times when I wanted and needed both constructive criticism and "rah rah" support, I would like to thank Ben and Brad Cordero for suggesting that Mac needed to be made more human and less a brain without personality.

Diane Williams, upon hearing me read chapter one, thought it needed to be two chapters. She was right.

Becky Lyons who was the only one to plod through my entire manuscript once before editing and once after, noting how much improvement there was from the one to the other.

Then there are the many who constantly asked how it was going and encouraged me to continue. The most vocal of whom were Delisa Marchetti, who knows something about being a published author, Chip and Karen Johns, Dave and Pam Kelps, Nina Bleu, Misty Anderson, and my niece Teri Baker.

There were those who gave professional guidance, chief of whom was my editor, Carol Crawford, who served as a mentor to me with her text corrections and nine pages of marginal notes. Our phone conversations were a wonderful classroom for this fledgling author.

Debbie Canon, whose advice I sought out as she is a published author. Besides her advice, she also gave me Carol Crawford's card. One of the best tips I could have gotten.

Olivia Beaumont, whose stunning artwork and professional opinion I value, was very helpful by giving me straightforward encouragement and realistic expectations.

I can't forget to acknowledge all of the helpful and friendly people at BookLogix. You didn't rush or pressure me, which made the pre-publishing process much easier. Thank you.

Lastly, in memoriam, I would like to acknowledge Gary Herrod. He was eager for me to get a little training. He gave me his college textbook on creative writing and, when he heard me read a portion of my manuscript, said that I had the talent to be a writer. Whether he was being kind or really meant it, I thank him and I miss him.

About the Author

Mr. Tuskey was born in 1951 in Wheeling, West Virginia, to hard-working parents who instilled in him the sound values of that generation. He received a comprehensive spiritual education and taught a public-speaking class for some twenty-five years.

He developed a love of reading in the ninth grade when his English teacher had the class read Dickens' *Great Expectations* and discuss it. His love of literature and his vivid imagination moved him to think about writing a story of his own. After several attempts, it culminated in a dream he had no intention of writing about—until he told his wife the dream. He now happily lives with her, approaching forty-six years of marriage, in a small town some fifteen miles outside of Savannah, Georgia.

Lightning Source UK Ltd.
Milton Keynes UK
UKHW022011101221
395433UK00010B/970